MESMERIZE

A Mystyx Novel

MESMERIZE

A Mystyx Novel

ARTIST ARTHUR

KIMANI
tru
™

Recycling programs
for this product may
not exist in your area.

MESMERIZE

ISBN-13: 978-0-373-53464-7

Copyright © 2012 by Artist Arthur

www.KimaniTRU.com

Printed in U.S.A.

For those who have had and lost love—
it's truly a mesmerizing ride.

Dear Reader,

I really enjoyed writing this installment of the Mystyx series. Lindsey Yi's struggle is different from the other Mystyx because it involves her emotions, as well as those of the people closest to her. With her past haunting her and the possibility of love on the horizon, Lindsey is walking a difficult path.

Mesmerize chronicles the growth of each Mystyx as they have finally come into their powers and face the evil that's been taunting them. It's a story of triumph that is long overdue for the foursome.

I hope you enjoy this leg of the Mystyx journey!

Dream big!

Artist

And remember, no matter where you go, there you are.

—Confucius

one

Useless Facts

My name is Lindsey Yi and I'm telepathic. I have been able to read people's minds for as far back as I can remember. I'll be seventeen in a couple of months and it's close to the end of my junior year in high school. I love cheese and absolutely hate ketchup.

I know that the diet of lady beetles consists of soft-bodied insects like caterpillars and that giant African crickets enjoy eating human hair. That's not necessarily something I need to know, but I have a reservoir of useless trivia like that stored in my brain for some inexplicable reason.

Another fact: It's been a year since the accident—twelve long months—since I've had a full night's sleep or experienced a waking minute of the day when I didn't think about my parents. I can still see their glassy eyes as they breathed the last puff of air in their lungs.

My entire body shivers as I rub my arms to soothe a layer of gooseflesh that coats my skin. As I close my eyes, I'm once again right back there, reliving the train crash one more time.

We were going to Washington, D.C. Dad went there a lot. He used to be a diplomat to South Korea. That's where he and Mom come from. I was born in the United States, but I traveled all over the world with my parents. When the accident happened, we lived in a huge house in Providence, Rhode Island.

I guess we could have taken a plane. But Dad liked to travel by land whenever he could, so we were on Amtrak sitting in business class. I don't know why, since I wasn't traveling on business. But I liked to pretend that I was a very important person in the government. That's what I want to do when I grow up, work for the government in some high-level international job. Sounds ambitious and probably obnoxious, but it's what I want to do.

My parents were sitting across from me, my dad with his laptop open as his fingers danced across the keyboard, and his eyes focused on whatever appeared on the screen. Mom was reading a book. She loved to read. Judging by the cover—with a bare-chested man and a woman with long red nails grazing his pectorals—it was probably a hot, steamy romance. That meant that mom won't be passing it on to me for my reading pleasure. That's okay. I prefer reading nonfiction, anyway.

My blunt-tipped fingernails—just like Dad's—drummed over the tabletop that separated us as I stared out the window. Trees whizzed by at a steady clip. Sometimes they were interrupted by water as we crossed a bridge. I was taking in the scenery but Dad wasn't, and it was his idea to take the train, anyway. I liked how the water looked like it shimmered, like there was a huge plastic coating over it that captured the rays of sunlight in a glittering spectacle. The trees made me think of shelter, of something hidden within the tall cluster of shrubbery with hundreds of outstretched arms on the sides. I didn't really want to think of those arms, grabbing, touching, pulling and tearing at me. That had always been a sore spot for me.

Then the scenery abruptly changed with such a jolt that it made me slide into the empty seat beside me. Dad's computer slid over the table, then bounced off the floor with a thud. It didn't sound good. Mom dropped her book, the pages quickly fanning out as it fell to the floor. I remember thinking, "She won't remember what page she was reading because her bookmark was still on the table." The book had fallen off the edge, too, resting on the floor beside Dad's laptop.

I grasped the armrest but the shaking didn't stop. I was quickly flipped right out of my seat, careening over the mess on the floor beside us, being catapulted somewhere inside the train car that I didn't know. Screams echoed in my ears and pain slammed into my body, even though I could have sworn I was floating through the car without actually hitting anything. Still, the pain was there, it was real and it was growing.

The right side of my head hurt like it had been smashed into something and throbbed furiously at the assault. My arms ached and there was a whoosh of air as I felt like something slammed into my stomach. I heard voices in my head, screams and pleas, amid the cries for help.

Outside the window, there were no longer trees or water, but an upside-down world that I couldn't really decipher. There was smoke billowing upward over the windows in clear gray waves. There was movement all around me, but I remained still. I swallowed as my body finally began to settle, and I cringed as the stinging taste of blood coated the back of my throat.

The cries in my head grew louder and louder and were now replaced by snippets that formed a chaotic sound wave that reso- nated through my entire body. My mouth opened because something wanted to come out, but I didn't know what. It might have been anything like, "Help me, I'm hurt." Or, "Save me!" Or, "I'm dying!" Or maybe even, "This pain is excruciating. Please some-one help me!" Whatever it was, it all came down to, "What the hell is going on?"

I couldn't say anything. It just played like a loop running through my head. I remember rolling over and coughing, since smoke was everywhere by now. Getting to my knees wasn't easy. My elbows rested on the floor, but there was glass everywhere so I lifted up my arms. I scraped away the tiny shards and saw the blood on my fingertips as it dripped down my arm and fell to the floor in red droplets. I got up off the floor and looked down to see that my knees matched my elbows, but there was no time to dwell on that.

"Lindsey!" a familiar voice called to me. "Lindsey, honey, where are you?" the woman said.

At that moment, I was thinking about how to form the words, but my mouth still wasn't working. My legs moved in a wobbly way, like I'd been thrust back to the days when I was a toddler trying to take those first steps. Lifting one leg at a time was a chore, one I needed to concentrate on. But the voices in my head wouldn't allow it.

I doubled over and suddenly felt like the glass on the floor was somehow embedded in my stomach. The pain was so intense, my eyes watered. And once again I tried to open my mouth to scream in agony. Still, nothing.

I'd been rendered mute and there was no explanation why.

Squeezing my eyes shut, I tried to breathe through the pain but it was relentless. My chest heaved as my head felt like it was going to split in two. Even my eardrums ached, like they did when I had that rotten tooth in fourth grade.

I kept moving, because in the midst of all the noise, I heard my mom's voice coming through loud and clear.

The chaos seemed to have quieted in my head, seeping out through my ears, spilling out so that it appeared to surround me. I felt myself being pushed and jostled, but I kept trying to walk, trying to get to Mom's voice. When I finally did manage to, I stopped. My legs gave out and I was back lying on a bed of broken glass on the floor.

Then I realized that my parents hadn't been thrown when my body ricocheted through the train. At the time I thought it was strange since we were sitting right across from each other. But it looked like they never moved, as their backs were still plastered to the faux-leather seats that are only in business- and first-class cars on Amtrak. Dad's laptop was definitely busted and Mom's book was gone. She'll have to buy another copy and start all over, I thought.

Her fingers were all bloody so the pages would probably get smudged when she opened the new book. Maybe she'd buy an e-reader instead, I thought. On one side of her head, the right side, there was a gash that oozed blood in thick rivulets that covered one of her eyes and trickled down to her lips. When I reached out to touch her, my arm ached so bad that I couldn't do anything but let it fall back to my side. Dad was next to her and his head looked fine. No blood. But his chest was moving up and down, in quick motions that didn't seem normal. Trailing down the bottom of his shirt was a gruesome crimson color. The blood was coming from his stomach.

I didn't reach out to him, but instead folded my bruised arm over my stomach to suppress the spasms and knife-sharp pains that were resurfacing once more.

"Dad!" The sound came from my mouth in a sick croaky-sounding way.

He moved his head slowly as the narrow slits of his eyes searched *for and then found me. He did like this hiccupping thing and blood gurgled from his lips. I cringed and swallowed, and felt like I tasted the same blood.*

I wanted to say, "Mom," but I couldn't. My mouth was already full. I looked at her, at her long, straight, jet-black hair that was now matted to one side of her face. She reached up to touch me. The sound in my head screamed, "Stop her!"

She froze in midair, as her arm hung aloft for a second then fell limply to her side.

I looked from my mom to my dad and my dad to my mom, back and forth over and over again. The pain coursed through my body making me tremble. I couldn't talk anymore, but I kept swallowing. I hated the taste in my mouth, hated the feeling of warm blood as it oozed down my throat. I kept staring at Mom and Dad, at their eyes. They blinked in unison. Then they stopped blinking and simply stared straight ahead, that empty soulless stare.

Death is final. It's the end and there's no coming back. No resurrection. It's over and done with. My mom and dad are gone and I'm still here.

These are the facts. I don't know if they're useless facts or not, but these are the facts.

two

True Dreams

JUST before my alarm is set to go off, I reach over and press the small black button on the clock to turn it off. This happens every morning. I always wake up before the alarm sounds, avoiding the loud buzz that will jolt me awake. Yet every night before I go to bed, I find myself checking the clock to make sure the alarm is set, just in case.

My mind is still a bit foggy with sleep, and my eyelids are too heavy to stay open for very long. The pillow is soft against the side of my face, and my breathing is muffled by the fluffy, goose-down fill inside. My bed is a full-size. So when I stretch, my legs don't hang off the sides, but instead are nestled under the pink-and-white-floral-printed sheets. But no matter how wildly I toss and turn through the night, I always wake up alone. The feeling of loneliness doesn't end when I switch off the alarm clock. It follows me throughout the day. No matter how many voices I hear echoing in my head, I know I'm still alone.

Pieces of my dream dance around in my head, filling my mind with questions. I see his face clearly from memories of last night's fitful slumber. He has dark brown hair—a little too long for a boy—curling around his ears and down his neck. He is tall and muscular for a teenager, but cute. However, it's his eyes that I really remember—deep, deep, blue, like the rarest sapphire or the view of the ocean from a tropical beach. And when he stares at me, he sees the real me.

To make it to school on time, I need to get up and get dressed. If I'm not in the shower by seven-fifteen, Mrs. Hampton, who is normally cranky anyway, becomes even nastier. Why my parents made Aurora Hampton, the sixty-year-old "wicked witch" of Lincoln, Connecticut, my legal guardian in their will, I'll never understand. All things considered, I probably shouldn't refer to Mrs. Hampton as a witch, I mean especially since I know that magicals and gods and curses actually exist. Sasha believes that Mrs. Hampton is probably my supernatural guardian, too, even though she'd never open her tight lips and tell me that herself. Of course, I'd never bother to ask.

The wood planks are cool under my bare feet as my soles touch the floor. Leaning back, I stretch and yawn and shake my head trying to clear thoughts of the cute boy in my dreams. It seems like a normal thing for a sixteen-year-old to dream about a boy, except that this boy has no name and I don't think I've ever seen him before. Maybe he's like my imaginary boyfriend since I don't have any prospects of a real one.

It's cool in the hallway, much cooler than in my bedroom. The weather here is so unpredictable, that I don't dare presume what it feels like outside. Come to think of it, the weather everywhere seems unsteady these days.

My stomach isn't ready to be up and about this morning

and grumbles as I close the bathroom door. Maybe my usual breakfast of yogurt and granola should be something a little more substantial like oatmeal. Mrs. Hampton loves to make oatmeal, that's why I normally eat yogurt and granola.

When the warm water from the shower hits my skin, I relax under the soothing spray. It feels so good, the heat raining over my body. Closing my eyes, I dip my head under the spray to wet my hair.

Mistake.

I see the boy from my dream again, his bright blue eyes and huge smile grinning at me. He looks like he's staring through a window. As I concentrate on the image, the background behind him is moving. It's moving pretty fast. My stomach flips and I feel a pang. I realize that I'm still on the train, still reliving the pain and misery of my parents' accident. The cute boy is there smiling. And he's not alone. Behind him I see two girls standing, holding hands and smiling as their faces come closer into view.

My heart's beating faster and louder like I'm next to a speaker at a rock concert. I don't like this scene, don't like that people are in my dream and they're smiling like this is a festive occasion instead of the worst day of my life. With all my might, I'm mentally trying to open my eyelids, so that I can see the here and now and not a painful memory.

I hear laughter now as the scene becomes blurry in my mind. As I inhale deeply, I smell what seems like nature— an outdoorsy scent that fills my lungs like air.

"You gonna pay this water bill?"

I don't know if it's the loud raspy croak of Mrs. Hampton's voice or the blast of cool air hitting every pore of my naked, wet body but my eyes fly open and the laughter and memory disappear, replaced by the image of Mrs. Hampton, with her signature scowl.

With that kind of start to my day, it's no wonder I'm in no hurry to get to school. But when I step outside, something in the breeze makes me lift my chin, and directs my gaze upward, heavenward. The sky's a dusky blue today, with the sunlight just barely peeking through the clouds this morning.

I live in this old, almost dilapidated house, which is surprisingly sturdy and not so bad once you're inside. Most days it feels like I'm just staying there temporarily with Mrs. Hampton. It's not as comfortable as my home in Rhode Island was, but not as empty as a hotel—that's kind of how I think of it. The house sits at the very edge of the Lincoln city limits. Off the back porch, about ten to fifteen feet, puts me at the edge of a grove of trees in my backyard. It is a dark and alluring place that I've never ventured into, but I seem to be always drawn to.

Walking down the winding road that leads to Reed Street—where the bus picks me up—I sense something around me. Nobody else lives out this far, but I still feel a presence. It's around me, maybe something from the past, or something yet to come. I can't really tell.

Krystal is the medium, so I doubt very seriously that what I'm feeling is some dead person's aura, even though it feels just as ominous. Things have been different—very different—in the past few months, I'd say.

For years now I've been able to read people's thoughts. It's not a talent I would have chosen for myself, but it's a gift. That's what Mom said and I believe her. Learning how to live as a normal teenager with that gift hasn't always been easy. But I thought I finally had a handle on it, until the accident.

A cool wind blows lifting my bangs away from my forehead and letting them flop back down again as the breeze passes. The fabric of the yellow sundress I decided to wear this morning, without too much thought, billows over my body. It's fitted across my small breasts then flairs at my rib cage, ballooning slightly around my slim frame. Standing a mere five foot two inches, I have Mom's short stature and Dad's slim build. The breeze whispers over my toes painted with black nail polish peeking through my open-toe flats. I come to a stop at the corner.

The color yellow represents optimism, enlightenment and happiness. In feng shui it's considered a yang color and evokes feelings of warmth, cheerfulness and friendliness. Yin colors like black are associated with protection and power. Together the two opposing forces—yin and yang—are interconnected and cannot exist without the other.

In South Korea women tend to wear subdued colors all the time. Me, I wear black when I want to block out everything—the voices and thoughts—and yes, the unsettling emotions that would otherwise drive me insane.

Today I guess that means I should feel enlightened, optimistic—maybe even happy. Not so, at least not thus far. All I know is that the moment I opened my closet my eyes landed on this dress. I grabbed it and added a pair of sunburst earrings to match. Usually I follow my intuition when I know it's *my* energy—not someone else's. But it's getting harder to tell these days with so much energy buzzing around me. My senses seem much more acute these days—like tasting the sea salt in the air and knowing that it's going to rain or the tremors I feel under my skin when high winds are approaching, and the seething anger of Pace and Mateo, who bullied Jake so mercilessly.

Today, as I watch the bus slowly come to a stop in front of me, anxiety settles on my shoulders, like tiny fingers dancing along my skin, following my neck and down my spine. As I step onto the bus, the sensation continues even as the confusion of voices and thoughts assails me. When I reach an empty seat, I pull out a pair of black sunglasses from the beat-up old backpack Mom used to carry her books in. Since the accident, I've carried it every day, as if it somehow keeps her close to me and alive in some way. Slipping on the shades I stare down at my nails. My cuticles are rough and unruly, and seem as if they are reaching for something, trying to send me a message. As I chuckle to myself, a voice echoes in my head. "It's saying you need a manicure." The voice puts me at ease as I smooth my rough-looking fingernails over the bright yellow dress.

The bus is coming to another stop when I look up. The school bus door opens to allow students to board. For some reason, my eyes are riveted on the front of the bus. He steps up the three steps, passes the bus driver, who has an overgrown, grizzly gray beard, and walks down the aisle.

I pull my shades down to rest on the tip of my nose. My eyes take in the fresh new sneakers, crisp blue jeans and bright white shirt, along with the dimples, cleft chin and straight nose that collides like a lightning bolt in the sky with sapphire-blue eyes.

I've seen those eyes before.

That prickly feeling finds its way to my stomach where it tickles my insides when his lips spread into a smile. Suddenly my yellow dress is proving to be a good choice.

three

Passing Notes

HIS name is Dylan Murphy. He's on the varsity football team, has been since he transferred here a couple of months ago. That makes him a newcomer just like me. The only difference is he's so popular you'd think he was born and raised here in Lincoln instead of being a transplant.

Everybody knows Dylan, everybody likes him—guys and especially the girls. I know *of* him but I don't *know* him personally. Today, he was on my bus, which is strange because I've never seen him on the bus before and I'm pretty sure he has a car.

Dylan sits behind me in first period AP English class. This morning that fact has me sitting up straighter and trying to act smarter.

For the rest of the bus ride I try to sneak another look at him. He walks right past my seat after staring at me until my neck is going to break or I'm going to fall off the seat ogling him. He's the first one to look away when he slides into one of the seats in the back of the bus. I turn back around in my seat and hurriedly push my shades back on. The ride is tense to say the least.

By the time I make it to my first period class, the fact that he's already sitting at his desk before I get there startles me. But then he looks up, our eyes lock and I'm right back in my dream. Only this time the train is gone, it's just him and me—me and Dylan Murphy, alone.

I don't know what my teacher Ms. Drake is talking about, and most likely half the class doesn't, either. We only have two more months left, so most of the students are not really focused on school. This is an honors class, so the majority of the students are seniors. It's small, twelve students in total. There are three rows of desks, and seven desks in each row, so some of them are empty. In the two desks beside me are Leesah Giveny on my right, and Patti Parkinson on my left. In the one behind me is Dylan.

This is the longest first period ever. Ms. Drake goes on and on about standardized tests and how we all have to pass them before we can graduate. My mind is more focused on the steady stream of heat flowing from my earlobe, down to my ankles. For the past forty-five minutes I've been fidgeting in my seat. I just can't seem to get comfortable. The hard surface of the chair seems to chafe against my skin in the most annoying way. My fingertips are all tingly and the nape of my neck has a damp sheen of perspiration.

I want to turn around. I mean, really, really want to just turn around badly and look at him again. Just to make sure it's him. But I know it is. I'm just about certain. I could never forget those eyes and that smile. I realize it's crazy, like in the movies when a couple's gazes lock from across a crowded room, their hearts immediately declare their love for one another—blah, blah, blah. Unbelievable, right? I'm inclined to agree. Yet, it's taking a force much stronger than me to keep my eyes glued to the blackboard behind Ms. Drake.

When I feel a tap on my shoulder, I almost jump out of my chair. My palms flatten out on the desk. And even though class is almost over, I've yet to open my notebook. My heart's beating wildly. My eyes—and only my eyes—are moving from one side to the other, to see if Leesah or Patti is tapping my shoulder to get my attention. Patti is immediately eliminated since her head of curly red hair is lying on the desk, with her eyes closed. Leesah's doodling something on a notepad with a bright pink pen. She's not paying attention to me, so it's safe to say she isn't the one who tapped me—which leaves only *him*.

Counting backward from ten slowly, I turn around and look over my shoulder. He's looking directly at me. He's not really smiling this time. Just the right corner of his lips is angled up slightly. His eyes get my attention. He looks down and back up at me and I'm still staring at him like I've swallowed my tongue. Not that I can break out into a friendly conversation in the midst of Ms. Drake's elaborate explanation of the graduation standards for the state of Connecticut. Then Dylan kind of nods his head and looks up then down again. Finally, I catch on and follow his gaze and the nod of his head the next time he looks down.

There's a small square of paper he's inching toward the edge of his desk with his finger. It's folded neatly and precisely. And as I watch him move it with his finger, it falls over the edge of the desktop. In what seems like slow motion, I turn in my seat enough so that I can reach out and catch the piece of paper before it hits the floor. As the paper falls into my palm, I instinctively look up at Dylan. He's smiling at me now, a smile that unnerves me, making me take a deep swallow as if I'm trying to down a spoonful of Mrs. Hampton's oatmeal.

I turn around and face forward again, clutching the folded square of paper in my hand. For several seconds I try to steady my breathing. I've never been passed a note in class before. Being the new girl doesn't really afford much opportunity to build relationships that would lead to note passing. Growing up, I was allowed to take gymnastics, which for the most part was my social interaction with girls my age. That lasted about eight years then abruptly ended just before I turned thirteen. I suspect it was because I came home crying when the coach made a comment about my race. Only she hadn't said it out loud.

My fingers move over the square piece of paper as I switch it from one hand to the other. When I feel my heart beating at its normal rate, I carefully unfold the note and open the sheet of paper in my lap. The first thing I notice is how neat Dylan's handwriting is—for a boy, that is. His perfectly lettered script looks like the alphabet border on the walls of a first grade classroom. It simply reads: HELLO.

I can't help but smile. The expression just spreads across my face without any effort on my part. The steady beat of my heart picks up and double-times just a bit. It's really silly that one word could spark this type of reaction. But it does and all at once I'm giddy at the fact that I've received my first note from a boy. I hurriedly claim my pen and scribble a return greeting of my own, adding a smiley face over the *I* in my name.

With an exaggerated yawn as I lift my arms—a technique

I saw in one of those teen cable channels—I drop the note with my reply onto Dylan's desk.

Ms. Drake's words are drowned out now that I know Dylan is just as aware of me as I am of him. I doubt he's dreamt about me, but I'm guessing he's not telepathic, either.

The bell rings before Dylan can give me the note back and since we both only said "hi", it might make more sense to just throw it away. But as I head for the door I see he's already passed me and is waiting outside by the locker, the not-so-neatly folded square of paper still in his hand.

I walk toward him because he's staring at me and for some reason my feet just decide to go that way instead of down the hallway to my French class.

"Hi," he says, with a slight nod that draws my attention to his dark locks that curl neatly around his ears. He lifts his left hand with the note inside as if to show me he still had it.

"Hi, again," I reply, and to my chagrin my smile widens across my face without reason. I hope it doesn't make me look too lame or desperate. I *so* don't want to look desperate.

"I'm Dylan and you're Lindsey Yi."

I nod. "Yes, I am."

He shrugs.

We definitely have the body language down pat.

"What's your next class?" I ask. It's getting late and he doesn't seem to want to say anything else. He just looks at me, which makes me more than a little nervous.

"Trig. Yours?"

"French."

"What do you do after school?" he asks.

I think about saying nothing, or "whatever you want me to be doing," but that would definitely sound desperate, which I am not. So instead, I clutch my books closer to my chest and answer, "Cheerleading practice."

About a month ago the answer would have been "nothing," but when Gemma Truesdale sprained her ankle, Olivia Danville, the captain of the cheerleading squad, invited me to join. First of the year, when I originally tried out she'd said my moves were too stiff, my smile a little stilted. Lie. I took gymnastics for eight years and have much more agility than the tanned and primped *popular* girls currently on the squad. But I didn't argue with her, it was their loss. Now, it seems, the tables have turned and Olivia needs me since their best shot at competing at the state level depends on executing killer pyramids and stunts and not just glossy fake smiles and perfectly teased hair.

"Cool. I'll be at football practice. We can talk afterward." He shifts his shoulders away from the locker where he'd been leaning and stands even closer to me as he talks.

I don't think that was a question. It sounded too confident and cocky to be one. "Ah, okay," I mutter, unsure how I like this presumptuous new guy, with the phenomenally cool eyes.

"Good. See ya later," he says, tucking the note we'd passed into the palm of my hand before taking off down the hall.

Just like that, he's gone. I'm trying to register why a feeling of loss is overwhelming me at the moment. As I walk toward my class, hurrying so that I don't end up in detention this afternoon instead of at cheer practice, I open the note. Dylan's written something else.

I LIKE YOUR SMILE.

It's in all caps, just like that. And of course, I'm smiling again.

That smile carries me down the hall amidst random chatter bouncing around.

I can't wait to get out of here, I'm so not feeling school today.

My mom's being a real bitch not letting me have my cell phone for three whole days.

Normally, I'd be close to manic with all the noise in my head. The thoughts of everyone I pass by, everyone I so much as glance at clutter my mind every day—except when I wear all black, or if the other person is wearing all black.

Today I hear random thoughts without paying much attention to who they're coming from. I'm riding some kind of high. It's like euphoria is carrying me along the hallway toward my class. My feet feel like they're barely touching the ground. In my hand the slip of paper feels as soft as cotton, a keepsake of the wonderful dream that I can hold on to at last.

Then I stop.

The voices lower to a dull whisper.

I remember that when I stood next to Dylan, and he looked into my eyes and I looked into his, I heard nothing. He wasn't wearing anything black today and neither am I. Well, the black toenail polish doesn't really count. So how could that be? I didn't hear anything when I looked at him. No voices, no whisper of his thoughts, no echo of emotions. Nothing.

Strange.

four

Unforgettable Names

"HIS name is Charon and we're the greatest threat to his total dominance. Our presence gives *good* the advantage over evil, which he's trying to spread across this realm. He was cursed by Styx for trying to betray her. She created us through weather anomalies that transmitted energy surges that gave us supernatural powers while we were in the womb," Jake says, and then takes a huge gulp of his soda.

Sitting beside him in the cafeteria, Krystal nods, her hair hanging down around her shoulders and her silver earrings sparkling in her ears. "That sounds about right."

"So how did you get these powers and not your parents?" Twan asks.

Twan isn't a Mystyx, but he's Sasha's boyfriend and Jake's boy or whatever guys call their BFFs. I knew at that moment Jake had sold us out. Well, I guess you can't really say he sold us out. Twan is sworn to secrecy, and he's promised never to tell anyone about us or the evil around us. And considering how attached he is to Sasha, I believe him.

Jake shrugs. "My dad said they knew the moment I was born what I would be. My mom was marked, too. She told me that Styx controlled the sun and the moon, and created the solar eclipse that spawned the energy surge. During the eclipse, power emanated from a ring of light surrounding the sun and the moon. That energy sparked the weather events that set off supernatural forces. Those conceived during these weather events are marked."

"So there are more Mystyx out there," I say. "There have to be. If your mom was one, that's at least one generation of Mystyx. And weather anomalies are becoming more frequent. It stands to reason that there might be others besides us."

"I would think there would have to be to maintain the balance of good and evil in the future," Sasha adds. She has just finished eating an enormous salad for lunch. It looked like an entire garden in her salad bowl, but she quickly ate it all.

"Right," Krystal chimes in. "We're here for this battle, this time."

Twan thought about it for a moment. "So the real question is, how do you beat this Charon character?" he asks.

"How do we defeat a centuries-old demon that lives in the Underworld?" I ask more for effect, just to see if it sounds as impossible as I think.

Sasha sighs. "There has to be something we can do. With all our powers combined, perhaps we can destroy him. Although I don't think he'll ever really be dead," she says.

"But we can exile him to Hades," I say, trying to sound optimistic.

"What in the world is Hades?" Twan asks. "I thought it was a person not a place," he continues, munching on a mouthful of French fries.

Sasha gives him a look that totally says *yuck,* and I almost laugh out loud because that's exactly what I'm thinking. Instead, I run my fingers along the scroll Jake found in his yard and lower my voice a bit more. The last thing we want is for someone to hear us preparing to do battle with a powerful demon.

"There are different layers of the afterlife. The Underworld is the realm of demons. Hades is the land of the dead. Trance is the place where you kind of linger, an in-between state before you die. You can linger there for ages," I explain.

"Sick," Twan says, taking the napkin Sasha offered to wipe his mouth.

"We can't go to the Underworld. But can Charon enter this realm?" Krystal asks Jake, who for one of the few times is not wearing a hoodie today. He has on a light green button-down shirt that highlights the light brown flecks in his eyes.

Jake has come a long way. Well, he's come a long way emotionally, since I haven't known him that long. But I know the struggles he's gone through. I know the pain and the strength it took for him to make his decision. I know because I felt every torrential emotion his body went through. Lately, that's how my telepathic power has manifested itself. I'm more of an empath now than a telepath.

Among the gazillion books I have stacked in my bedroom, lately I've acquired an interest in Greek mythology and all things mystical. Now, of course I love my useless facts, but what I really love is when I read something that's supposed to be a myth or a legend and yet it's true. Like this whole thing we're mixed up in—the River Styx and us being Mystyx, and this gatekeeper guy, Charon, and the dark demons populating the town of Lincoln—parallel worlds of the past colliding with the present.

"I can travel to other realms," Sasha says.

Jake was already shaking his head. "You can't travel to the Underworld. And if you could, I wouldn't let you go alone."

"That's right," Sasha says, scooting closer to the table. "You know how to get there, don't you?"

"You do?" Twan asks. "Man, this is deep. Some days I just can't believe this is real."

I guess it would be hard for him to believe since it wasn't actually happening to him, just around him. And some days I wondered how we managed to keep the secret. Twan is the only outsider who knows about us. For years things have been happening around this town that are weird, and sooner or later people are going to start asking questions. People like Sasha's father and Walter Bryant, the local meteorologist, and now the police, who were still searching for the missing teens from the religious retreat.

Krystal finishes up her lunch and drinks the last of her Sprite. She looks like she's about to say something and then she stops. Her gaze moves toward something behind Twan's shoulder. She pauses, her entire body going still. Long, ebony hair frames her face, making her complexion look even darker. She has wide brown eyes with a naturally smoky eyelid that supermodels would kill for. Right now, all of her features are taking on a surreal effect as she continues to stare.

As if on cue, everyone at the table stops talking. We

know what's happening and are just waiting for Krystal to say something.

"Something's happening. Everyone who can cross over is doing so very quickly. The ones who can't are being hunted, their souls devoured by something dark and dangerous," Krystal whispers. Trembling fingers go to her face, grabbing strands of her hair and tucking them behind her ears. "They fear the darkness. They fear the evil it brings with it. With each soul it devours, it's getting stronger and stronger."

"Strong enough to walk this realm?" Jake whispers without taking his eyes off Krystal. "Charon's gaining power even without my help."

Jake has been unhappy that he is unable to thwart the demon by himself. It was a tough decision to let the good in him prevail over evil and even harder for him to accept that he was a vortex—a rare mix of powers of good and evil. I could tell him that he's on the right path and that his mother is probably happy that he chose good, just as I'm sure the rest of us are. But Jake's more complicated than just words. I could tell him all that, and he'd still carry that guilt around with him like a backpack. So I don't say anything, I just look down at the scroll, trying to figure out more of what it said.

"So how do you guys gain power?" Twan asks. It seems his voice has broken into Krystal's trance, because she gasps and stares down at the table. Jake immediately wraps an arm around her.

"Maybe I need to go back to the Majestic, find someone there who'll tell us what to do," Sasha offers.

She's worried now, we all are. The tension is thick as

thoughts of a world gone totally dark, powers still as yet un-leashed and places we'd never seen before swirl around us. With each breath I absorb more and more of the thoughts and feelings of the friends surrounding me. Krystal's heart is beating erratically, but Jake's touch provides some com-fort. Sasha's nervous energy is bubbling up inside of her so much so that she could barely stand still. Twan is anxious. I guess because he's on the outside looking in, that offered some measure of comfort. It's like a video game to him. As for me, I don't really have time for my own emotions. I'm so overwhelmed by everyone else's that my temples start to throb.

I'm so happy when the bell rings that I want to practi-cally scream. Instead, I take slow breaths, steadying myself before I stand up. I'd learned the hard way that I could be quickly overloaded by other people's emotions. Nobody in the group really knows about my empathic abilities yet. They're just getting used to the idea that I can read their minds. The only thing that stops me is black. The depth of color blocks everything out. It seems that every time Jake, Krystal or Sasha sees me, they're trying to block me from reading their thoughts by dressing Goth.

Despite my casual demeanor, Jake knows something's going on with me. I've picked up on it a few times, the way he looks at me, the questions swirling around in his head. Like now, he has his arm around Krystal but his eyes are probing me. He's asking if I'm okay, not verbally, but I can hear him clearly.

I nod and look away, grabbing the scroll and putting it into my purse. I don't like that he senses these things, like he can read my mind. Oddly enough, I don't like it when someone else tries to do to me what I routinely do to them. This whole situation is strange—my life, my circumstances, their lives, our predicament, everything. I can hardly think of anything else for the rest of the day, which is bound to be reflected in my grades.

"Lindsey can make the bottom four like Gemma used to do."

Olivia's voice is nasal and grates like fingernails against some imaginary chalkboard in my head. When I look at her I'm not at all surprised that her thoughts mirror exactly what she's saying. Nothing's going on inside her head except for cheerleading—like she's obsessed with this stuff, which is pretty pathetic. This is like the third time I've asked myself why I'm here. I don't like Olivia or girls like her. Yet I've voluntarily joined her band of dumb groupies.

There are ten of them making up the twelve-member cheerleading squad. James Ryerson is the only male and he's just a spotter. He's sitting on the lowest level of the bleachers as we're all standing just outside the gate that blocks the bleachers from the field. I guess once we get it together he'll come over, but for right now he seems content to sit there picking at his fingers like they're much more interesting.

Nicola Cronan and Davanna Lang are standing right beside me. They're both taller than I am and already wearing the short white skirt and yellow-and-blue-letter sweater. I'm just wearing shorts because I don't have the official Settleman's Chiefs cheerleading uniform yet.

"She's so small," Nicola says, looking at me like I'm a blade of grass under her sneakers.

"But that's where Gemma was in formation and she's

taking her place," Olivia says, sounding like she's whining for a new bicycle instead of giving a command to the pep squad.

"She might be okay," Davanna offers, giving me a small smile as she speaks.

I've seen her before, she's actually in one of my classes, math, I think. She has a pretty smile with perfect white teeth—definitely a product of braces. For the most part she's quiet in class but that could be because there were no other members of the cheerleading squad there. When I walked out of the locker room and across the field to meet them she'd been chatting happily with Nicola and another girl on the squad, all three of them yapping and giggling until Olivia blew her whistle, which I assume is the call to attention.

"Actually," I say because I'm not about to stand here and bicker all day over something so simple, "it makes more sense if I top the tower because of my slight build. You want your sturdier girls on the bottom to keep us steady."

Olivia looks at me like I've just spoken German and I know she's about to say something else but Coach Delaney appears from like nowhere. I didn't see her approach but here she is with two girls on either side of her, two girls who look insanely alike.

"Excuse me, girls, but I need to interrupt," Delaney says.

She's a tall woman with skin the color of dirt and a dingy gray-tinged ponytail that hangs down her back like the end of a witch's broom. Her face is fixed in a permanent scowl, sort of like Mrs. Hampton's. Even when she talks her lips remain turned down. It's a creepy look that sort of fits her and those wrinkled sweat suits she likes to wear.

"Isis and Ivy Langhorne are new to Settleman's. Just moved here, from where'd you say again?" she asks the girl on the right.

My first thought is that the girls are identical but when I look directly at their eyes—which I do out of habit since that's the way I read minds best—I see there's the difference. One of them has tawny brown eyes and the other has blue. Not as pure a blue as Dylan's, but still blue. This is only like the kazillionth time I've thought about Dylan since I've been out here, even though I'm trying valiantly not to think about him at all. That's really hard since I know he's just across the field running plays with the rest of the football team.

"We've always been cheerleaders." A crisp female voice draws my attention back to the girls and I see it's the blue-eyed one speaking. "I'm Ivy," she continues then smiles, a slow mechanical movement that doesn't touch her cool stare at all.

"Hi, Ivy, I'm Olivia, captain of the cheerleading squad here at Settleman's," Olivia says, stepping forth and extending her hand to Ivy, who doesn't even look at it, let alone reach out to shake in response. Olivia's arm drops to her side and she clears her throat. "Unfortunately, the squad's full for the year. You can try out next year, though. I'd love to see what you've got."

"We're seniors," the one named Isis says and her voice kind of echoes on the air.

Delaney interrupts then. "It seems there are two girls on your squad that failed Chemistry last quarter." She talks as she looks down at her clipboard. "Shannon and Eliza, you'll have to sit out the rest of the year. Everyone needs to maintain a C average in all classes to participate in a sport."

"But—" Shannon is already sputtering in protest. "I studied for that chem test. I really did."

Eliza isn't brokenhearted at all, just shrugs and marches right past Delaney without another word. That might have something to do with the college guy she can't stop thinking about. High school cheerleading probably pales in comparison to hot nights with an older guy. Not that I know anything about that, but Eliza definitely does.

"So Ivy and Isis are in, and Shannon and Eliza are out." Delaney taps her pencil against the clipboard, does an about-face turn and waits only a beat for Shannon to flock beside her where the twins just stood. Without looking back she begins walking, Shannon on the brink of tears right behind her.

The twins stay, both with picture-perfect smiles resting an equal amount of about three seconds on each girl before finally landing on me. Knowing how it feels to be the new girl I step forward and say, "Welcome to Settleman's." I don't extend my hand because I have no desire to have it left dangling in the air as Ivy did with Olivia.

"Well," Olivia says with a huff. "Let's get started. Lindsey's going to top the pyramid. Isis and Ivy you two can bottom on either end. James!" she yells. "Let's go!"

James pops off the bleachers like a jack-in-the-box and jogs over toward us. Ivy and Isis fall in line with what Olivia just said and we begin to practice.

I never did like the cheerleading squad much. The solitary craft of gymnastics holds much more appeal. But I'm trying to fit in here, to for once, actually belong. Since I doubt Mrs. Hampton will ever leave this small town, I won't be transferring to another school. This is home, at least until I head off to college next year. I might as well make the best of it.

And as if that thought reaches out into the universe and taps him right on the shoulder, Dylan stops midstride and looks over to me. Of course I'm looking over at him. I've been sneaking glances over there all afternoon. Our eyes lock, across the field, on a beautifully sunny spring afternoon and I think I could actually like it here in Lincoln after all.

five

The Long Ride Home

IT'S three minutes after five. I have precisely seven minutes to make it from the gym, out the front door and onto the bus stop. If not, I'll be walking the ten or so miles to my house. The late bus leaves at exactly five-ten. It's supposed to take home all the students who stay for after-school activities. Before I had no need to take this bus, now I guess I do.

The moment I push open the front door I choke on the dry heat. We practiced outside and it was warm but suddenly if feels suffocating. Reaching back, scooping my hair up off my neck, I fan a little then walk down the steps looking for the bus. It's not there.

I check my watch and frown as it's only six minutes after. No way the bus left already. As I walk down all the steps and head down the walkway despair rises. There're no other students out here waiting for the bus. Crap, I missed it. The idea of walking in this heat is not appealing. I wish I had a license and a car like Sasha, or a driver like Sasha. Even Jake has an old beat-up pickup truck that his father helped him fix and get on the road. It used to belong to his grandfather who died just a few months back. Neither of them are here right now to offer me a lift.

I'm just about to start walking when I hear a car approaching. There's only a small street that leads to the school then you have to turn into the circular driveway and either circle all the way back out to the small street or turn left and head toward the even smaller parking lot. But it's late so the only vehicle coming up here would be the bus. Turning hopefully, I'm only slightly deflated as I see this shiny black car with tinted windows approaching.

It's slowing down as it gets closer to me, sunlight glinting off the sparkling silver rims. I should keep going, after all, I don't know anybody who drives a car like this. Sasha has a red sports car that her bodyguard Mouse used to drive all the time. Now Mouse drives this huge SUV that looks like it could haul the entire cheerleading team if need be. And like I said, Jake's old truck doesn't compare to this shiny new toy at all. I think Krystal's mom just bought a new car, but it's a totally domestic sedan. Nothing like this. They're the only people I know in Lincoln.

The car stops and the driver's-side door opens. For that second the air cools, sweat evaporates from my skin and the despair of having to walk all the way home melts away when I see his smile, his eyes.

Dylan Murphy is the driver of the cool car.

"Hey, Lindsey," he says, walking around the hood of the car.

He's got a great body, muscled legs that fit his jeans perfectly and just enough broadness across the shoulders to make the button-down shirt look like it belonged to him and not his dad. His hair's wet, like he took a shower after practice, curling slickly around his ears and brushed back off his forehead.

"Hi, Dylan," I finally manage and pray the dorkish sound I hear isn't really my voice.

"Need a ride home?" he asks when he's close enough for me to smell his soap.

It's an intoxicating scent that gives me goose bumps. I push my book bag strap farther up on my arm to keep from reaching out and touching him. I really want to touch him which would push me past dorkish to sluttish in about a millisecond. "I was waiting for the bus."

"It's gone," he answers simply then pulls the strap from my shoulder taking my book bag and heading toward the passenger-side door without another word.

I have to actually command my feet to move. It's a silent command so Dylan doesn't think I talk to myself as well as stand outside waiting for a bus that's already gone. I probably shouldn't get in his car I'm thinking as I pause at the open door. I just met him this morning. He's been here for months but nobody really knows him or his family. I know because I asked a couple of girls about him throughout the day at school. The consensus is he's a stranger, a newbie— even newer than me—but a hottie just the same. I kind of felt cool that I'd changed notes with a hottie before any of the other girls at school did, at least I think that's the case.

"Come on," he says after putting my bag in the backseat. "I won't bite you. It's just a ride home."

I look at him and wonder, he is exceptionally handsome and this car is as hot as he is. That should spell serial killer or possibly vampire. I've seen that in the movies. And now that I know the impossible is definitely possible, my heart beats just a little faster.

Then he smiles and the debate is over.

"Sure," I say and step toward him. "Thanks."

"My pleasure," he says, waiting as I slide into the cool leather seat and instantly reach for my seat belt.

"Let me get that for you," he offers as he leans over me to snap the seat belt in place.

I hold my breath, which is sort of silly since I'm already in danger of fainting—hot guy, cool luxury car, hot spring afternoon—a deadly combination.

"Thanks," I say, with a whoosh of air.

He kind of stays there hovering, his face only inches from mine.

"You have pretty eyes," he says and I'm all flustered. I don't know what to say next.

Besides, my eyes are just regular brown and of course they're slanted or "chinky" as some of the more ignorant students of Settleman's call them.

Anyway, a compliment's a compliment. So I clear my throat and mutter, "Thanks." Again. I sound like a tape recorder. "So do you."

Yeah, just what every guy wants to hear, his eyes are pretty. Just shoot me now.

But Dylan's smile just widens and he pulls out of the car and closes the door. Inhaling and exhaling quickly I'm trying to calm myself down. The interior of this car smells brand-new, fresh leather, cool air blowing from the vents. It's spotless and spit shined like he just cleaned the inside and out. When he climbs into the driver's seat and clicks his own seat belt he turns the radio up and we pull off.

I know the song that's playing, "Can't Get Enough" by Black Eyed Peas. I don't know if it's appropriate or not but Dylan turns it up louder and I smile because I really like this song and we're riding around Lincoln like we own the town and all seems perfectly well.

Until he stops at the bottom of the hill where my house is. Suddenly the lovely mood dims and I feel like sliding out of the car and carrying myself slowly up the hill to the haunted house. That's what the kids call the house I live in. They say Mrs. Hampton's a witch and she boils animal heads to make spells to cast against the townspeople. It's an old rumor that I hear has circulated forever. I remember when we went on the hayride, Pierce Haynes told a similar story of Mrs. Hampton's witchcraft skills, as well. But I live there and nothing happens in that house, haunted or otherwise.

"Thanks for the ride," I say when he turns down the radio. I'm already unbuckling my seat belt and am about to reach into the backseat for my book bag when he touches my arm.

"I can pick you up tomorrow," he says.

"Really?" I ask. "Why were you on the bus this morning if you drive...this?" I ask for lack of a better word because really this is like twenty steps up from riding the yellow, public-school transportation bus. I'd been thinking this while we were riding but didn't want to interrupt him listening to the music, he seemed to be enjoying it. And I have to admit I did, too.

Mrs. Hampton isn't big on me playing music in the house, says it has subliminal messages in the lyrics. Yeah, I guess if you're listening for crazy stuff like that you might hear it, but if you're just listening to music that's probably what you're going to hear, as well. To keep the peace I plug my earbuds in every chance I get in the house without her seeing them.

"It was in the shop. I was glad when I got the text that the car was waiting for me after practice. I was not looking forward to the bus ride home, except for the fact that I would have gotten the chance to see you again." The dimple in his chin makes him look older, sexier.

And I can't believe he just said he wanted to see me again. Or at least I think that's what he just said.

"So your family has a lot of money?" Wow, that's rude. I can't believe I said that, especially since I'm not what the Lincolners call poor. Their class system here is weird, segregating people by the section of town they live in first, then by the size of their bank account. I try not to get caught up in all that but Dylan's circumstances seem a little strange.

He laughs instead of being offended and I'm relieved.

"We're okay," he says. "Me and my sisters all have our own cars. That way my dad doesn't have to cart us around all the time."

"Oh," I say. I guess that makes sense. "Your sisters go to Settleman's, too?" I didn't know Dylan Murphy had sisters.

He nods. "We're all seniors."

My look must have said "that's also strange" because he clarifies quickly. "We're adopted."

"Oh." I really like repeating myself around this guy.

"So I'll pick you up tomorrow?"

Great, now he probably thinks I have the vocabulary of a third grader. I sigh because there's no way of making this better without making it worse. So I just shrug and answer, "Sure."

His smile is back and the happy that's supposed to center around the color of my dress is blooming. "See you tomorrow," I say, then make myself move.

He touches my arm, stopping me as I try to pass him. "I'm glad I took the bus this morning," he says.

"Me, too."

His fingers are featherlight on my arm. Still, there's this heat radiating throughout the limb and combined with the temperature outside, I'm afraid I might actually melt.

"See you tomorrow."

I nod and move again. This time my arm slips from his grasp, his fingers tracing a heat path along my skin before the connection is lost. Walking up the hill, my legs feel like dead weights and actually threaten to turn around and go back to him. But I continue staring forward not wanting to know if he's leaning against his car staring at me walk away. Secretly, however, I hope he is!

When I finally get to the front porch I do chance a look down the hill. The slick black car is still sitting there glinting in the fading sunlight. And Dylan's leaning against it, legs crossed at the ankles, arms folded over his chest.

With fluttering fingers I wave, then let myself into the house only to sink to the floor with a gushing sigh that just might have been disgusting should anyone have walked by to see me.

SIX

Dark As Night

I don't like the night. Never have. That's true for various reasons, but tonight it's because I can't sleep. The past couple of months have been a repeat of insomnia. I'm either having the nightmare about the train crash or I'm up walking the floors. Tonight, it's walking and I end up outside near the water once more. The moon's just a slither of gray in the dark-purplish-colored sky. No stars, but I never see them anyway so it's nothing to be missed.

I thought I'd slip into slumber easily tonight with visions of Dylan dancing merrily in my head. Corny, huh? Yeah, I guess so. That's probably why I'm walking out here listening to the constant rustle of water rippling. Dylan seems nice, a little mysterious, but still nice. I've never liked a boy before, not really liked the way Sasha likes Twan or Krystal likes Jake. And for a while, I've been feeling like the third wheel with those two couples even though they don't exclude me, especially from their thoughts.

The last time I was out here the moon was huge and it was blue or it had a bluish tint. There was something in the air that night, something I'd never felt before. Until now.

There's no breeze but the air around chills all of a sudden, so much so that when I breathe out my mouth, frost smoke billows in front of me. My arms instantly prickle with chill bumps and I lift my hands to rub them. I keep walking with no real destination in mind. Actually, there is a destination—toward this feeling.

It's a deep longing, like something inside me reaching out for whatever is out there. Through the taller grass and patch sand/dirt mixture I keep walking. The feeling's stronger now, my breath pants with the effort of containing it because I'm not walking fast at all. My gaze stays in front of me even though it's really hard to see anything, it's so dark out here. Dank air filters through my nostrils as I press against memories that threaten to distract me.

The wind stirs and whips my hair around my face. Usually this would bother me, the many wisps itching my fair skin. Tonight, I don't mind. Nothing can break my stride, nothing can stop this longing ache that seems to be headed toward its sweet relief. My chest rises and falls, up, down, up, down, steady breaths producing a steady heartbeat that grows louder and louder as I get closer.

Above, the tall branches of trees bend and whine in protest to the wind's powerful pull. I step right into the forest without a care what may be beyond the perimeter. It's even darker here and something scratches my cheeks, bare arms and stabs into my feet. But I keep going.

I can't stop. It's calling me, pulling me, needing me.

A great gust of wind howls in my ears just before knocking me flat on my face. Twigs dig into my face and the palms of my hands as I scramble to get up. It's relentless, this wind that's whipping so strong around me until I feel like I'm inside a funnel cloud. The only difference is I'm not being sucked up, but pressed farther into the Earth. I cough out a breath trying to breathe. It feels like something's standing on my back, pressing me down, down, down. My nails dig into the ground snapping twigs, scraping against hardened dirt and I open my mouth to yell but no sound comes out.

Now I think I should be afraid, I should be ready to get up and run as fast as I can from whatever is going on deep in this forest. But the longing's still there, the feeling that something wants me here, that I belong here is even stronger, like a huge lump in my throat pressing its way down. Trees are breaking, falling to the ground with a loud rumble. The ground shakes with an angry burp and I struggle once again to stand. It's a futile effort, I'm just not strong enough to fight against this wind. At least I think if I could just stand, to actually hold my head up and see what's going on, maybe I could get away. All I can manage is to turn my head but that motion earns the stark pain of something cutting across my face. Tears burn my eyes as helplessness takes over and tiny edges of panic outline my mind. I'm going to die here in the middle of the forest, wearing only my NY Yankees nightshirt.

Just as I think death is imminent, something wraps around my ankles and begins to pull. Now, I'm being dragged and every part of my body screams. Every part except for my mouth that acts handicapped against yelling for help. Air puffs out of my mouth in thick streams as I'm quickly flipped over and dropped onto my back. Again, I can't scream but my eyes are wide open and I'm almost blinded by a burst of light then what looks like drizzling fire. Instinctively lifting my arms to cover my face, I inhale the distinct stench of burning flesh and feel vomit rising slowly, swirling around like hot liquid in my throat. I remember that smell from the train crash as people around me endured burns from fires that ignited afterward. It's a sickening smell and has tears streaming down my face.

Then I'm yanked from the ground. My whole body jerks with the force as something picks me up until my feet aren't even touching the ground. We're moving now, quickly through the forest with that smell still lingering in the air. The wind isn't blowing and it's now infernally hot; my bangs stick to my forehead and my nightshirt, which is twisted all around me, is damp.

We're moving fast now. Me and whoever it is that's carrying me. They have me by the collar of my nightshirt, my back to them so I can't see who or what it is. I don't weigh a lot but we're moving as if I weigh absolutely nothing, so I'm guessing it's a what that's carrying me and not a who. That is so not a good thought. Trees blur past us, a cool breeze whipping my hair back and my nightshirt up. Behind us is a loud roar, like a volcano erupting. The cool air is suddenly swallowed by thick heat that has sweat sprinkling along my skin. In a voice I think is familiar, I hear low chanting.

"Dark as night, large is fright. Take away this beast tonight." Over and over the raspy voice says as my body jostles in its wake. I want to turn to see what's carrying me, or who's talking. I want to see what's going on.

Then the sky rumbles with ferocious thunder, and lightning bolts reach down touching the ground just in front of us and on the sides of us.

The chanting grows louder, "Dark as night, large is fright. Take away this beast tonight!"

Maybe if I said it, too, it'll work. But my mouth's still on strike. With each inhale my insides burn from the heat ingested. Tears stream from my eyes steadily, fear eating a gigantic hole in my chest. Everywhere the lightning hits, a small fire rises until we're practically surrounded by flames.

"Lindsey!" Another familiar voice sounds in my head. I know this one for sure. It's Krystal. I know she's not here physically but I hear her just the same. She's a medium so she can communicate on different plateaus than normal people can. I know she can talk to the dead and pray I'm not one of them and that's why I can hear her so clearly.

"Think of your power, Lindsey. Think of our power combined. Think. Think," Krystal's voice urges.

Then the raspy voice speaks. "Feel, Lindsey. Feel what's inside of you growing and growing. Feel the power."

Feel. Think. Feel. Think. How am I supposed to do anything when I'm scared out of my mind, my skin being singed from a small distance, my eyes blurred with tears? Then flashes from the train crash rip through my mind. My mom's eyes, the blood trickling down her temple. My dad's grimace, his arm clutching his stomach. Then Mom smiling as she finishes cleaning my great-great-grandfather's dagger, which he reportedly received from the spirit of the sea umpteen hundred years ago. Dad's laughter as we watch an episode of *King of the Hill*. Dale was his favorite character.

There is a feeling inside me and I will myself to focus on that alone. It's pain and its like an incessant burning in the pit of my stomach. Closing my eyes I wrap myself completely around that pain, embracing it, touching it even though I know the consequences. It burns the edges of my mind like newspaper catching fire. The singeing heat stings and yet I keep concentrating, keep focusing until there's another blinding light. I see it even though my eyes are closed. I feel it in the tingling freeze against my skin. We're moving again—me and whoever is carrying me—through the cold.

When I open my eyes again I'm lying down and there's quiet all around me. The familiar tan wallpaper with tiny burgundy pineapples on it that matched the god-awful chairs is the first clue as to where I am. Inhaling deeply, the scent of cinnamon permeates the air and I almost feel comforted.

"She's awake," someone says.

"Finally," another female voice adds.

They're both pretty close to me because I hear them clearly but up 'til now, I've only ventured to stare at the wall and the ceiling. With slow motion because my head feels like it can explode at any minute, I turn to look at them.

"Krystal," I say and am amazed because now my voice decides to work.

"Hey," she says with a tentative smile.

"Hiya," Sasha chimes in as she squeezes beside Krystal so I can see them both.

They're both smiling but it's a strained smile. They seem to have on their pajamas and that just doesn't make sense.

"Why? Where? How'd you two get here?"

Sasha nods her head toward Krystal. "She had a vision and she called me. I picked her up and we came right over."

"A vision?" I ask, slowly pulling myself up. A wave of wooziness hits me and I drop back down.

"Take it easy, you've been through a lot," Krystal says, adjusting one of the huge throw pillows behind me.

Sasha puts one under my feet and squeezes her butt on the edge of the chair there. Krystal just stoops where she is, putting all her weight on her knees as she looks down at me.

"I was in your vision," I say because I already know the answer, just want to hear what she has to say.

Krystal nods. "You were walking along the beach real quietlike then out of nowhere this beast rose from the water and grabbed for you. But before it could take hold of you, another beast grabbed you and carried you away. The water beast was coming for you, stretching long dark water arms onto the shore to get you but you were steadily moving out of reach. Your chest, head and ankle looked like purple lightbulbs were beneath your skin, glowing and leading the water beast directly to you through the dark of night. I figured you could stop the light if you just thought about it, about whatever was going on to cause it. I tried to send you a message." She shrugs. "Did it work?"

I nod then stop because the action is not helping my headache. "I heard you. You told me to think."

"That's right. I did." Krystal looks at Sasha, who only shakes her head then back at me.

"Now you tell us what happened out there," Sasha says, rubbing my leg and sounding like a concerned mother. It's weird hearing Sasha sound like this even though out of the four of us she's the bossiest one. Still, tonight her voice sounds different, somberlike, adultlike. Her pajamas are deep green, a silky material that almost shines. It's pants and a top, and over the top she's wearing a jean jacket.

Behind her is the big bay window that overlooks the side
of the house where there's a big hill that would probably
be great to sled down on a snowy afternoon. And why I'm
thinking that at this very moment is beyond me. Maybe
I'm scared to think about what happened. That's a definite
possibility.

"I couldn't sleep," I say slowly. "No matter what I did I
just couldn't sleep. It seems like it's been that way forever."

"You try counting sheep?" Krystal asks with a hint of
humor in her voice.

Sasha's shaking her head, the ponytail she's pulled her
long brown hair into sways with the action. "Casietta swore
by warm milk. It worked for me every time," she offers.

Now I hear the warmth in her voice, feel the dull stab
of how much Sasha misses their former housekeeper. She
hasn't mentioned her much in the months since Casietta's
disappearance. I wonder what's brought her up now, but
don't dare ask. They're here to figure out what's going on
with me, not the other way around.

I sigh. "I'll try the milk next time." Sasha smiles and I
feel a little better knowing that my words made that happen. "So I was walking by the water. I do that a lot when
I can't sleep. Nothing ever happens when I do."

"I remember when I walked by the water one time, a
spirit almost scared my dinner right out of me," Krystal says.

They're trying to make me feel better, trying to calm
me down even though they have no idea what I've been
through or what memories are haunting my mind. I guess
that's what friends do. Since I've never had real friends before I don't really know for sure, but it's a good feeling that
they're here, anyway.

"I wasn't afraid at first, just lonely, I think. And then there was this feeling, this need and I followed it. I just walked where it led me. I didn't think about where I was going at all."

"And you ended up in the forest?" Sasha asks.

I nod. "I remember the twigs cutting me." Then I look down at my legs and my arms to see how much damage was done. There's nothing there. Reaching for my cheeks I feel smoothness.

"Nothing," Krystal says quietly.

"It stung. Each time another one dug into my skin it stung like hellfire. I wanted to scream but it wouldn't come. Then I fell and something was holding me down, pounding on my back like it was trying to drive me into the ground like a stake or something." I shiver involuntarily at the recollection.

The room is so quiet. Sasha and Krystal are staring at me waiting for the next word as soon as I speak my last one.

"I can't get up but finally I roll over, then something grabs me and lifts me up. We're running and running and then there's fire, a circle of fire and we're trapped."

"And you use your powers to get out," Krystal finishes, putting her hand on top of mine that's been stiff over my stomach for the past few minutes.

"I don't know." I'm shaking my head, which hurts like the devil as I try to figure out exactly what I did or didn't do. "I don't have any active powers, just the telepathy."

"And the empathy," a voice from across the room says. "She's an empath you know."

It's Mrs. Hampton and we all look over at her. She's standing in the archway, an eerie yellow glow from all the candles she keeps lit in the foyer providing a haunted-looking background. She's wearing a floral robe—I swear she has a million of these god-awful ugly things—and house slippers that could use a good washing or a blow torch. Her hair's all over the place. It's a dusty brown mixed with gray and this other odd-looking copper color. It looks like a condemned bird's nest. In her hand she's holding three satchels by the ties letting the dark bags hang at her side.

She knows what I am, what we all are. I had a feeling she knew but in her tight-lipped nature she never said a word. Until now.

"You're an empath, too?" Sasha asks.

I shrug even though I know. "I've been feeling all kinds of things lately."

"You've always had the ability, you just blocked it," Mrs. Hampton says as she comes into the room stopping at all the windows and pulling down the blinds, flipping them up so no light can get in. Beesley, the big scruffy-looking dog that's always lounging somewhere in the house, lets out a strangled yelp as her slippered foot catches the end of his tail. "Now it's time to unblock it and get down to business."

Me, Sasha and Krystal exchange questioning looks because Mrs. Hampton has never talked to them before and has only said the mechanical greetings and references to me in the time I've been here. Tonight she's talking as if we've known each other forever. Totally strange.

When she comes over to the sofa and plops a fat hand over my forehead I almost scream again. She's never been this close to me and never touched me before. But now her fingers splay into my hair, her eerie green eyes staring down into mine. "You feel right as rain now, I bet. It was a test and you passed."

She drops one of the satchels onto my chest then tosses one at Sasha and at Krystal, who fumbles a bit before holding hers in the palm of her hand.

"What is this?" Sasha asks, weighing hers from one palm to the other.

"It's heavy," I say and look at Mrs. Hampton.

"It's the key to your powers. Open it," she directs.

We all open our pouches and pull out what looks like river rocks at the exact same time. The heat starts first at my fingertips then simmers down to the palm of my hand where the smooth gray rock slides. "It's a rock," I say as if nobody has figured that out yet.

"From the goddess's river," Mrs. Hampton says. "The Guardians hold them until the time is right."

"You're my Guardian?" I ask in awe. Sasha loved her Guardian and so did Jake. We all just assumed Krystal's Guardian was her mother since she obviously knows about Krystal's powers, but so does Jake's dad and he's not a Guardian. This isn't making any sense.

Mrs. Hampton nods quickly. "I was given yours to pass on to you tonight."

Krystal looks on skeptically. "You knew we'd be here tonight?"

"I knew the test was coming. Just as I knew she'd need help. Yours and mine. And Styx's."

"Wow, rocks from the River Styx," Sasha says, still looking down at hers. Then all of a sudden she looks up. "That means you've seen Casietta. She's alive, right? She's somewhere safe and alive. She left because of my dad, but you can tell her that he's gone now and she can come back," Sasha says, looking really hopeful.

Mrs. Hampton keeps her lips tightly closed, but shakes her head negatively. None of us really know what that means. Or we know but don't want to know.

"So who's my Guardian?" Krystal asks.

"Who does not matter," she snaps. "You will know when you need to. What matters now is only that you have the tool to do the job."

"What about Jake?" I ask, almost afraid she's going to bite my head off for daring to ask. Why'd I have to get the moody Guardian?

"He has what he needs. Now you do, too. Use it when the time comes."

Then as quickly as she'd appeared in the room, she's gone.

"Typical," Sasha says, rubbing a thumb over her rock. "They can never just spill everything all at once."

"Probably for a good reason," Krystal says quietly.

"So it's testing me now?" I ask, looking toward the covered windows wondering if the water beast is still out there, if the next night I couldn't sleep and wandered down to the lake it would jump at the opportunity to claim me.

"All of us have been tested," Krystal says. "I guess it's your turn."

Her words make me shiver. My entire body's cold except the hand where I hold the rock. "Then what?"

"Then we'll be ready," Sasha says. "For Charon and whatever he tries to do to us."

She sounds so dire, so deadly calm, yet serious as anything we've ever heard before. Krystal looks contemplative and ready. I guess it is my turn, time to do my part. I can only hope I'm ready.

seven

He's Not My Boyfriend

When Dylan and I pull up in front of the school, everybody seems to stop what they were doing and stare.

A cluster of richies stand near their cars, two girls and three boys, they all stop talking and look at us as Dylan opens the door for me and I step out of the car. Five steps and they're finally behind us so I can't see the questioning or hating eyes pinned on me anymore. Because even though my dad was like government famous, I'm still in a lower rank here in Lincoln because I live in the old haunted house with the town witch. What else could I expect?

There's a group of Trackers who just stepped off the school bus. Jake used to ride that bus but since he has his own wheels now, he picks Krystal up and they ride to school together. I didn't see his truck in the parking lot so I guess they're not here yet. It's okay, I promise myself, even though I don't have the Mystyx here to have my back, I'm okay. Dylan is holding my hand. I'm better than okay.

As we approach the steps that will take us into the side door I see familiar faces and almost weep with joy.

"Hey, Linds," Sasha says, walking right up to me and Dylan.

"Hi, Sasha," I answer, even though we're sharing a look that's holding a much more personal conversation.

With raised eyebrows, Sasha wants to know who Dylan is or more likely why he's with me. With a big smile I answer he's mine.

Twan reaches out a hand to Dylan. "Hi, I'm Twan. You're on the football team. Saw you sack those two players from Bridgeport last week. That was tight!"

Dylan shakes Twan's hand with his free one. His other hand is still comfortably holding mine. "Dylan Murphy. Thanks, glad you're a football fan."

"Wow, Lincoln sure is getting a lot of newcomers all of a sudden," Sasha says. "You haven't been in town that long, right, Dylan?"

I hear the words spoken and catch the doubt that's lingering in her mind simultaneously.

"But you don't have any problem making friends," Twan comments with a smile my way. He's thinking of how we look good together. I smile back because I like his thoughts a lot better than Sasha's right now.

"Where'd you move from, Dylan?" Sasha asks.

"We're from up north," is all Dylan says and even to my own ears that sounds cryptic. But maybe he's just not in the mood to be interrogated. I mean, really, it's barely eight-thirty in the morning.

"Hello, people. Ready for another exciting day of eleventh-grade academics?" Krystal asks when she and Jake approach.

"Dylan's a senior," I volunteer and feel like a dope for

saying that so quickly, especially since everybody already knows.

"You must be Dylan," Krystal says with a wide-eyed stare my way then a level smile to Dylan.

"Hi," he says.

Jake looks at him and I instantly worry. Jake's still the edgy one of our bunch. He has a knack for being easily agitated even though I think he's making strides in the area of anger management, especially after he denounced the dark nature of his Vortex heritage.

"We have gym together," Jake continues.

Dylan nods and he and Jake shake hands.

Jake doesn't like gym. Well, he didn't a few months ago when Pace and Mateo were being total bullying goofs. Now that Mateo's gone, Pace just seems sullen and doesn't really say much to anyone. The consensus between us is that Mateo had been possessed by Charon's demonic henchmen, which made his bullying of Jake magnify to like the hundredth power. But when Pace backed down from the bullying and Jake stood up to them both, Mateo was destroyed. We suspect Charon wasn't happy with his failure. Mateo's parents reported him as a runaway, which was strange since they knew he'd come into the library with them to ride out the hurricane. It's like they didn't want any questions asked about his disappearance, and at the same time didn't really care enough to want to find the truth themselves. People are weird like that in Lincoln.

"Right," Dylan says to Jake. "We should get going before the bell rings," he says, looking at me.

"Sure. Okay." I clear my throat. "I'll see you guys at lunch."

They're all looking at me as I walk away with Dylan. Man, that was awkward standing there like I was in front of a panel that would decide the fate of me and Dylan. Even though there technically is no me and Dylan. Is there?

Chemistry is not holding my attention at all today. All I can think about is Dylan's hand in mine. Dylan opening the car door for me this morning after picking me up on the corner. Dylan walking me to second period class since we're in first period together. I guess what I'm saying is all I can think about is Dylan.

Never thought I'd be that girl. You know, the one who sits in class and doodles his name all over the papers in my notebook. Or the one who gazes off into space, all thoughts centered on this one guy who may or may not be thinking of her the same way. I read about these girls in books and see them on the gushy chick flicks in the movies, but never related to them the way I do now.

I can tell I'm becoming one of them by the extra twenty minutes it took for me to get dressed this morning. And my outfit, it's pink, not a color I usually wear. It's the quiet color of universal love. Pink carnations mean "I will never forget you."

See what I mean, I'm officially that gushing teenage girl on the brink of love. And that's normal, right? Something I never thought I'd be.

From the outside looking in I'd probably gag. But being right in the middle, front and center, I just feel this wonderful glow that I hope isn't on display for everyone around me.

Then there's the one dark spot in my life right now. The

memories. I should be finished grieving and I think I am. I mean, I'm not lying in bed crying all day like I did the first two months after my parents' deaths. I miss my parents like crazy, miss the life we used to have. It usually seemed pretty hectic, but it was all I knew. Some days I feel like I'm breathing different air than I had a year ago, becoming another person entirely. That scares me because I never thought the old Lindsey was so bad.

At least I can get up every day and function in this new place, which is a great feat, said my old psychiatrist, who used to come to the house to see me because Mrs. Hampton didn't want to take me all the way to Hartford for office visits. Still, I think about the accident constantly, wondering why it happened and how I was the only one to survive—without any injuries at all, except for the broken heart.

The circumstances surrounding the accident were equally questionable. After months of investigation there was no one to blame. The train was in excellent condition as were the tracks. Nobody knew what it hit or what may have caused the crash and explosion. It just happened. A freak of nature, some of the papers said. Another unexplainable event, more concluded. Me, I just don't know. But with each new dream or nightmare—I guess is more accurate—I get the sense that now, a year later, somebody's trying to tell me something.

A shrill ringing jars me from my thoughts and I sit straight up in my chair on alert.

It's a bell with a different kind of ring from our normal changing-classes sound. It's loud and screeching and vibrating the windows so that they rattle in the walls. Mr.

Beveridge looks astonished one minute, then astute and in charge the next.

"We've had fire drills before, children. Let's move swiftly and quietly to our designated stations."

Settleman's has designated fire stations so that wherever you are in the building you're to follow the color strip on the floor in that hallway to the desired location. I've already grabbed my purse, leaving my books on the desk and am headed out the door and into the hall full of bustling teenagers eager to be leaving class even though the reason is a possible fire.

This could have been a drill but normally that's stated over the PA during the morning announcements that a drill will take place sometime during the day. Today there was no announcement.

I'm in the green group and our location is at the back of the school where the parking lot is. Jake and Sasha have Spanish this period and their class is right down the hall from mine, so they're in the green section, too. We meet up and all look toward the building.

"What do you think is up?" Jake asks first. "It doesn't feel like a drill."

"No," I add. "It doesn't."

"There!" Sasha says, pointing to a second-floor window in the corner of the building. "Smoke."

She's right, there's thick rings of smoke billowing through the window, which means there's really a fire in the school. We're obviously not the only ones to notice this because there's an eerie kind of silence as we all gather outside. Normally there's a lot of chatter and the teachers are going up and down trying to keep us together like a herd of sheep. Today, even the teachers are staring up at the building in awe.

The fire department's sirens are blaring at this point as they get closer to the building. My chest heaves as waves of panic whip through me. I'm scanning the crowd so bits and pieces of dozens of thoughts at a time are rolling like a steamboat through my head. There's fear and shock and panic rising. Clasping a hand to my throat I try to swallow, to get a grip on this overwhelming feeling but it's getting worse, fast.

"It's the culinary class," Twan says, stepping up to us and standing near Sasha. He's wearing straight-legged, dark blue jeans today and a New York Knicks jersey. Not black, so his thoughts of dread are now washing over me like a fresh waterfall.

I stumble back against Jake who hurriedly asks, "You okay?"

I'm nodding my head, but I'm not speaking. I can't. Again. And that's enough to make me even more nervous.

Looking away from Twan doesn't really help. There's someone to the right of me that's on the phone with her mother, I guess, and she's near tears telling her the school's on fire. To the left of me there's a guy holding his cell phone up in the air to record the smoke billowing out of the window now in a steady black stream. I was going to turn away but I look again.

The smoke is black, not gray as it was before.

"It's him," Sasha whispers.

Jake takes a step closer to me then I hear Krystal's voice.

"It's worse around the front of the building. They said

it's the entire C hallway. The fire department will try to contain it," she reports like she's a newscaster.

Her heart's pounding in her chest, I hear it in my ears like there's a microphone attached to her. Suddenly I can't breathe, I'm choking from nothing. The smoke hasn't reached us yet and the sultry air is becoming second nature. But something's lodged in my throat. It's sitting perfectly still holding my breath hostage and my eyes water with the effort.

Jake grabs me around the shoulders. "Lindsey, you okay?" he keeps asking but his voice sounds distant.

Krystal comes around the other side, pushing my hair back from my face. Sasha's fanning me with a piece of something she picked up from the ground and Twan says he'll go try to find me some water. But none of that's going to help.

It's too much, the emotions, the sensations. I hear everything, every voice in the vicinity. I feel even more, every thought and concern rippling through me until they're crawling beneath my skin like beetles. My eyes close and I want nothing more than to fall to the ground and sleep. Sleep and never wake up. That's the only way I'll get rid of all this inside of me, inside of everyone.

Then the smoke thickens. Out of the corner of my eye and just before I collapse to the ground I see a huge plume of black smoke explode from one of the windows. Glass shatters and kids are screaming and running away from the building. The scene is utter chaos at its best. Then the smoke sort of pauses right in the air, regroups and charges directly at us.

"Run!" Jake yells and pulls me by the arm behind him.

Krystal has me by the other arm and Sasha's right beside us. All of us run. I don't know how I make my feet move when all I want to do is stare at this big blob that's following us. Everybody's running now and screaming. Firemen are reaiming their hoses but they're moving in slow motion, I suspect because they've never seen smoke take aim and attack before. When I turn I look right at it. I mean it looks like a face, a distorted beastly face with fangs and eerie red eyes. It reaches out for us, for me, with long clawed hands and I open my mouth to scream. I hear the sound but know it's not coming from me.

Sasha and Krystal are screaming coupled with all the kids running alongside us.

My warm skin tingles when sprinkles of cold water make contact. There's a steady trickle. Is it raining? No, it's the firemen, they're aiming those hoses directly at the smoke, which is now baring its teeth, its hot breath on my back, blowing my hair. It's just like last night, this rush of emotions, the running, the fear. Krystal said she'd seen a water beast. This is a smoke beast. I'm betting they're one and the same.

I stumble and fall to the ground, my arms slipping from Krystal's and Jake's grip. And the beast is right there, centering its heat over me.

I can't move, am paralyzed with my cheek pressed to the concrete. Then I'm being pulled up, again, just like last night.

Only this time I see who's rescuing me. I see his beautiful blue eyes.

eight

My Hero

Dylan holds my hand as we sit on the curb. His thumb is making tiny circles along my skin causing me to shiver.

"It's okay," he says. "The firemen have it under control now. They said it was just a grease fire."

"A grease fire in a culinary classroom with an electric stove that only has one working burner," Jake says sarcastically. He doesn't believe it was just a fire.

Neither do the other Mystyx. I have to agree with them. But Dylan doesn't need to know that.

I squeeze his hand a little to let him know I appreciate his words.

"They should just let us all go home," Dylan says.

He's looking around the school, all across the front lawn and down the circular driveway where all the students and teachers are still standing or sitting. We'd run from the back of the building when the smoke beast had come after us, only to be stopped around front by firemen and policemen.

"They want to question us," Krystal says. She's sitting on the other side of Jake.

We must look like a helpless bunch, all six of us sitting

and staring at the building that now has black scorch marks on the bricks around the upper windows.

"They think someone set the fire," Twan says. "They weren't even cooking in culinary today, just doing some bookwork." When we all look at him quizzically he adds, "I ran by Nancy Gilliam when I was looking for her water. She said they weren't cooking but all of a sudden there was all this smoke. They just got up and ran out of the room."

"So somebody's trying to burn down the school. I wonder why," Sasha contemplates.

"Seriously, because we only have a few weeks left until summer break. It's not even that serious," Twan answers because he's not listening for Sasha's real question.

"It's no big deal. We'll get out a few weeks early. They aren't teaching anything new at this point anyway," Dylan speaks up. He's not staring at the building but looking at me. "We can head to the pool when we're finished here. Make the best of an early dismissal."

It's not a question. I blink in confusion because yeah, I'm a little confused. I'm still trying to get a grip on what happened. The fire drill, the smoke beast chasing me, waiting to be questioned by the police—basically everything that's taken place in the past twenty-four hours. But Dylan doesn't know any of this so I guess his suggestion makes sense.

"That's a good idea," Twan says. "We can all meet up at the pool."

Jake doesn't seem thrilled with that idea. He probably wants all of us to get together to brainstorm our next step, which really, at this stage needs to be something. I'm getting really tired of running.

Two uniformed officers approach, their scuffed black

shoes making a muffled sound over the asphalt. My eyes still burn a bit from the smoke as I look from their shoes to their black-clad legs up to the light blue shirt with the bright silver badge over the left pocket. They've been in Lincoln all their lives, they look really comfortable here. I feel like I've been in Lincoln a lot longer than a year, too, which is weird considering my past of traveling and never quite getting totally settled. Maybe Lincoln is where I was supposed to be all along, with the other Mystyx.

"We'd like to talk to each of you, one at a time," the officer who's more built than the other one says. He's older with his graying temples and frown lines around his eyes. He's also looking directly at me.

So I stand up because he wants to talk to me first. He thinks I look out of place, the only Asian in this group. It's funny how some people still look at me like I'm a foreigner when I was born right here in America just like they were. I've always tried to keep an open mind about ethnic prejudice believing that it's the other person's problem, not mine. Today, I still kind of feel that way because he's thinking I'm an outsider because I have Asian blood and Asian features, but he has no clue how different I really am.

I walk toward him without saying a word and he turns to lead us away from the others. Krystal got up to talk to the other cop and they move in another direction. Glancing around I see the crowd's thinning. Some parents have come to pick up their kids. The local news van is here with its sole reporter and cameraman standing close to Principal Dumar's car talking to him. I don't look up at the building.

"Did you see anything near the culinary room today?" the officer asks right away.

"I was in chemistry class on the first floor. I didn't see anything but the smoke."

He nods his head thinking he should believe me but still hesitating. "You were outside when you saw the smoke?"

"Yes."

"Didn't see anything unusual as you were leaving the building?"

"No."

It's easy to answer simply when you're telling the truth. I don't know what these question-and-answer sessions are designed to find out because every kid is probably saying the same thing. We were in school enduring one of the last days when we heard the fire drill. We got up and walked out like we normally do, then a huge smoke beast attacked like none ever has in Lincoln. He doesn't ask me about the smoke or if it had a face, which is probably good considering I probably couldn't answer that as simply as I do the rest of his questions.

"You can go," he says but as I turn to leave he shouts, "What's your name?"

He's holding a notepad and a pen, which probably holds close to a hundred or so names of kids and teachers alike. With a shrug I figure its harmless enough, besides, he's the authority figure here. "Lindsey Yi."

As I walk away I feel like he's still watching me, trying to figure out what to think about me. Any other day in any other town, if I were any other teenager I might think that was strange. But as it stands, my life is becoming stranger by the minute.

My bathing suit is black. It's cut out on the sides and snaps in the back and around my neck. Modest and slightly sexy, I'd say. It's the last one Mom bought me before she died.

"You're growing up, my Lindsey," she'd said with that wistful look in her eyes.

Every time I think about Mom now she has that look in her eyes. Even when she's smiling. It's like she knows something is coming, something she's dreading. Did she know she was going to die?

That's a depressing thought and today I've had enough of the unusual and distressing. It's time for some fun since we had the early dismissal from school. Tying a black sarong around my waist and slipping on flat black sandals, I grab my bag with a change of clothes, sunscreen, house keys and cell phone and head downstairs to grab a water from the fridge. Dylan's picking me up in about fifteen minutes. I know he won't be late.

"You should stay inside," Mrs. Hampton says ominously the moment I walk into the kitchen.

"It's too hot to stay in." I don't really want to talk to her. Well, I do, because I have lots of questions for her, but the look on her face—as usual—says she's not up for answering them.

"You've had a busy day," she says, folding her beefy arms over her chest.

Walking past her I pull the refrigerator door open and wonder while the cool air hits my face, why I was blessed with such a surly Guardian. There's no way my parents could have been friends with this woman.

"I'm not hiding from whatever is after us. If it wants me it can come to the pool and get me."

"Don't think it won't."

"Then so be it," I snap and hope I have this much gumption the next time that beast stares at me.

"He wants your soul. You can see others' minds. He needs that power to help him rule. He'll hunt you until he has you."

"I'm not going willingly," I say, really glad that she's at least giving me something to go on. "And besides, I'll have the other Mystyx with me."

Mrs. Hampton nods her head. "You are more powerful together. But there's a piece you'll have to fix on your own."

I figured as much. I'm the new one in town, the newest one to the Mystyx and my power is different from the others because it involves other humans. Krystal communicates with ghosts and Sasha's astral projection puts her on a plane with magical beings. Jake has the most physical power with his telekinesis. But my power is more solitary, more mental. I'm sure there's a reason for that and lately I've been thinking that it has something to do with my parents' deaths.

"How do I fix anything without an active power?" I ask once I have a bottle of water in my hand and close the refrigerator.

"You figure out what it wants from you and you make sure it knows it can't have it."

Okay, this sounds like Jake's battle. He's a Vortex, that means he has good and evil power in him. Charon wanted him to turn pure evil, Jake chose to remain good. So Charon is still after us. But what do I need to choose and how do I do it?

I know one thing for sure and I tell Mrs. Hampton in no

uncertain words. "If he wants my soul he's going to have to kill me for it. So all I have to do is stay alive, right?"

Mrs. Hampton shakes her head. Beesley eases his way into the kitchen moving at a pace too slow and too comical for a dog its size. His big paws slap the linoleum as if he can barely stand to take another step. Then he plops down right beside Mrs. Hampton, his preferred spot.

"He wants what you have inside you, what you can do with what's inside. That's what he wants."

"How much did my parents know about this?" I ask just because I keep thinking about the way Mom used to look at me.

One of Mrs. Hampton's hands finds Beesley's head and rubs. Beesley breathes heavily, sounding like this might be his last breath. "They knew what was coming."

As she says those words my cell phone chimes from inside my bag. The sound startles me and I jump a bit then dig inside to retrieve it.

"Hello?"

"I'm out front," his deep voice informs me and I'm instantly warm all over.

"I'll be right out," I say but don't really want to go. I want to stay and talk to Mrs. Hampton some more since it seems like, despite her disdainful look, she's actually in the mood to tell me what's going on.

"I'll be back in a few hours. Is that okay?" I ask because she's kind of strict on my comings and goings and the times thereof.

"I don't like that boy," she says with a frown.

I frown right back in response. "Who? Dylan? You've never even met him."

Then her free hand moves to her neck, to the huge piece of rock she wears on a dingy old string. "I don't get a good feeling," she mumbles. I wonder if her rock is from Styx like ours.

"Do Guardians have special powers, too?"

"We have the ability to be what we need to be when we need to be it. That's why we were chosen to guard you."

I know Dylan's waiting and I should really go, but I ask one last question. "You were chosen and told who to protect. Or did you choose who you wanted to protect?"

Mrs. Hampton looks up to me, her dull eyes latch on to mine and I can't move a muscle, it's so intense.

"I knew from day one I would be with you."

My cell phone chimes again and I start to back out of the kitchen. "I'll be back."

"By eight o'clock," she says. "It loves the dark and after showing itself in broad daylight today at the school it'll be hungry for more action. Keep your stones close and your mind alert."

I nod, then run back upstairs to grab the small satchel of river rocks she'd given me last night. My feet barely touch the steps as I hurry back down and out the front door. Dylan's not out front, he's down the hill and I almost ask him why he couldn't just pull up in front of the house and come in. Isn't that what boyfriends do?

nine

Pleasure Interrupted

The pool's not as crowded as it usually is. It's not quite four o'clock yet but I suspect most of the kids from school are at home, still reeling from what they saw. We're not because it's becoming second nature for us. I don't think Dylan saw the smoke. He acts like he didn't and I don't really want to talk about it anymore so I don't bring it up.

We all drop our towels and bags on available chairs and sit while we lotion down. Dylan's wearing black trunks that reach his knees. His legs are hairy and so is his chest. I find it really hard to swallow when I look at him. Without all his clothes on he's even hotter than I originally thought, with muscled arms and ripped abs that look like he should be modeling in a teen magazine instead of walking the halls of Settleman's High.

"Here, let me get that for you," he says, taking the bottle of suntan lotion from my hands and sitting behind me on the lounge chair.

I sit right on the end because I put my bags up top. Dylan spreads his legs and scoots closer to me. I jump when I hear the top snap open. And when his hands touch my skin I feel like I'm going to burst into flames. Seriously, the heat that erupts from his touch to my skin is intense and I blink, thankful for the darkness of my shades so nobody else can see the complete shock I'm experiencing.

Closing my eyes I picture how we must look. Two dark-haired teens sitting at the pool in bathing suits, one massaging suntan oil into the other. It seems a lot more intimate in my mind than I think it looks. I mean, after all, we are at the pool. Cracking open my eyes when I hear talking around us I realize Jake's doing the same thing to Krystal and it doesn't look that intimate. But Krystal probably feels different. It's all about the feeling. I'm getting that now.

"I really like your suit," Dylan says in my ear and it takes all the control I have not to jump right out of my skin.

His breath whispers over my skin and suddenly I want nothing more than to be in the pool.

"You guys are taking forever," Sasha says as she comes to stand right in front of me.

Her bathing suit is a shimmering gold configuration of ties and swatches of material that aren't covering all that much of her bronzed body. Twan's walking behind her, his dark trunks a sharp contrast to his girlfriend's glittering ensemble. At first I couldn't see the connection with them, but now it's evident. Twan totally gets Sasha and everything she's really about. Sasha really likes him for that, for seeing past the outside and respecting what's on the inside. Now, I find myself rooting for their budding love all the time.

Dylan snaps the cap back onto the bottle and says, "All done."

I stand up and untie my sarong then slip my feet out of my sandals. The sun's still shining bright when I look up to the sky. There're no clouds, the day is clear and beautiful. For now.

We all head for the water, slipping into the coolness slowly, then splashing about, afterward playing made-up games until we're all exhausted from the effort. We get out of the pool then go and sit in the hot tub.

That's when I notice the two girls at the bar staring at us. One wears a white bathing suit, a two-piece with a silver swirly design that looks a lot like symbols or something. The other's wearing red, it's a one-piece but it's cut high up on her thighs and the back is completely out, save for the slip of material barely covering her bottom and the snap at her neck. They're both blonde with hair cascading down their backs and they wear huge sunglasses that cover the entire upper half of their faces. But I know they're looking at us, they have been for a while now.

Dylan's arm around me as I scoot over on the bench next to him pulls my attention from the girls and back to him. He hasn't stopped touching me since we got here. I'm getting used to it now so I don't jump every time he does it, but I do notice that Sasha and Krystal are paying a lot of attention to us, as well. I don't know what the big deal is. So I didn't have a boyfriend when I first arrived in Lincoln. It's been months, can't I have one now? All right, I really need to stop calling Dylan my boyfriend because we just met. But he's totally acting like a boyfriend so why shouldn't I act like a girlfriend?

I snuggle closer to him the way Sasha and Krystal do with their guys and we talk about school and our plans for the summer and next year.

"I've already started sending out applications," Jake is saying.

"Really? You still thinking of going to Columbia?" Sasha asks as she scoops her wet hair into one hand then drapes it over her shoulder.

Jake clears his throat before he talks. He's becoming a lot more sociable now with all the changes in his life. "Thinking about staying closer to Dad now that he's all alone. I applied to NYU and Towson State."

"I may go to NYU, as well. I'd like to return to the city," Krystal adds.

"Everybody has a plan," Sasha says kind of quietly.

"I don't," I chime in. "I mean, I know I want to study political science or something like that but I don't have a clue where I want to go to study it."

"You've been everywhere," Krystal says. "And your grades are perfect. You can have your pick where you go."

She's right but for some reason what she's saying sounds wrong. I shrug. "I just don't know. Haven't really thought a lot about it lately."

"I'm going to Atlanta. Depending how my SATs look I may try for Clark. I'm taking some SAT prep courses this summer."

This is Twan talking and Sasha splashes water as she turns quickly and faces him. "I didn't know you were thinking about leaving Lincoln."

"My grandmother wants to move down there with her sister because her husband's sick or something like that. I'm not letting her go alone," he says solemnly.

Twan's a really good guy. But Sasha doesn't look happy

about his announcement. It's Dylan who directs the conversation elsewhere.

"So where do you go to party in this town?"

Twan smiles despite Sasha's sullen look. "Now you're talking," he says. "There's this club, Trends. They've got a sick DJ and dancing. You have to be eighteen to get in but I've got the hookup with one of the bouncers. If we're there before eleven on Friday he'll let us in without ID."

Dylan nods. "Sounds like fun. You in?" he asks me.

I've never been to Trends or any other club for that matter. Mrs. Hampton's not going to be crazy about that idea.

"Come on, pretty girl, you remember you had a good time when you met me at Trends?" Twan prods Sasha until she's cracking a smile.

"It was okay," she says and I know she's trying to hide how good a time she really had because she wasn't supposed to be there and it was the first time she'd astral projected anywhere.

"Do you think your mom'll let you go?" Jake asks Krystal, whose mother has been more and more into the church lately so she's probably not going to go for the idea of her underage daughter going to a club.

"I don't know," she replies.

"Hey," Sasha says, perking up a bit more. "Why don't we have a sleepover on Friday at my house, that way neither one of you have to worry about whether or not you'll get permission."

This is a good thought since Sasha's basically unsupervised with her mother in like some kind of trance since her father's been out of town and her housekeeper/nanny is gone.

"That sounds good. I don't think I'll have a problem ask-ing to go to a sleepover," I say, thinking that Mrs. Hamp-ton, who has turned out to be my Guardian, will probably think we're together planning our strategy against Charon and his madness.

"How about you? You think you can go to Sasha's?" Jake asks Krystal. She looks a little leery but then nods her head and the planning begins.

The guys are going to pick us up at Sasha's at ten. Well, Jake and Twan are. Dylan said he has something to do early in the evening and he'll just meet us there. I'm a little dis-appointed that our three-way date won't start off with all three couples together, but I'm still psyched that I'm a part of a three-way date in the first place.

The afternoon progresses and we end up at Maggie's ordering cheeseburgers, fries and milkshakes. Even Sasha bites into a big greasy cheeseburger, smiling as she knows her mother would have a cow if she could see her. I'm so happy right at this moment, so content being a teenager in this small town with these great people I can now call my friends.

But that good feeling is short-lived.

I spot the two girls from the pool again. This time they've taken a table across from ours. And yes, they're staring again.

"Do you know them?" Krystal leans over the table and whispers to me.

"No. But they were at the pool earlier. I've got this feel-ing," I say then let my words trail off because I can't really explain the feeling. It's not like I'm reading their minds or their emotions for that matter because I'm wearing black, which pretty much blocks me from the assault of others' thoughts. But it's something else, a new feeling that I'm almost certain is not welcome.

"Here, have a bite of my burger," Dylan says, pulling my attention from the two girls.

I frown because his burger has a bunch of stuff on it that's making the bread soggy enough that everything's sort of sliding all over the place.

"No, thanks," I beg off and reach for a fry instead.

"Chicken," he jokes and we resume our comfortable banter between each other.

All in all it's been a good day, if I forget about the smoke beast chasing me and the two weird girls following me with their eyes. The end of the evening is best of all.

Dylan drives me home, stopping at the bottom of the hill as he likes to do. I'm too tired to even question him as I unclick my seat belt.

"I guess I should have asked you this before." He starts talking like he doesn't see I'm getting out of the car. "But are you seeing someone?"

"No," I answer too quickly. "I mean, I'm sort of new here, too, so I really haven't had time to meet a lot of people."

"Really? How long have you been here?"

"It'll be a year in September."

He nods. "I don't like being the new guy. I've been new before and I don't think it's cool."

I chuckle. "It gets easier, believe me. Plus, being on the football team helps. You're instantly friends with all the jocks."

"Yeah, I guess you're right. You're a cheerleader, so that gives you a lot of friends."

He looks sort of thoughtful at this moment, like he's talking but trying to figure something out at the same time.

"I just started that this week. Krystal, Sasha, Jake and Twan are the best friends I have here in Lincoln. They seem to like you," I offer.

He kind of shrugs and I wonder if that means he couldn't care less. We're quiet for a few minutes after that. You know the awkward kind of silence when two people are trying to figure out what to say to each other. We don't know each other all that well for conversation to flow freely but I feel like that could be a possibility.

"You hang out with the others a lot, huh?"

I guess he's calling the Mystyx plus Twan the others so I answer, "Yes. They're the first group of kids I really connected with since I've been here." Which is absolutely true. "You don't like them, do you?" It's just an instinct but he doesn't talk a lot around the "others," he sort of concentrates only on me, which could be considered a good thing. But I'm getting this weird vibe from him where my friends are concerned.

He shrugs. "Not really my type of friends."

Hmm, don't know how that makes me feel—should probably give him points for honesty, though. "You asked about partying and Twan suggested the club. What was that all about if they're not your type of friends? I mean, you are going to Trends, aren't you?"

He nods and the golden glare from the street light a few feet away from us reflects off his hair and the side of his face. His perfect face.

"I'll definitely be there on Friday," he said matter-of-factly.

It's not much but I smile because I'm glad he intends to be there. After today I like the three couples and have no desire to go back to being the fifth wheel.

"Well, I have to go," I say, and attempt once more to leave. Dylan's hand on my arm stops me.

"Come here," he says and his voice is kind of husky.

I lean over closer and can smell the product he uses in his hair. His eyebrows are thick, his nose only slightly crooked. He tilts his head and I instinctively do the same.

"Close your eyes," he whispers and his breath is a warm breeze over my face.

Everything inside me is tense, eager, anticipating. My eyes flutter shut and a millisecond later I feel his lips on mine.

Enchanted is the word that comes to my mind. Everything about this moment is enchanting. The deep indigo sky, the sleek shiny car, the beautiful, mysterious new guy, completely enchanting.

Dylan pulls me closer, deepens the kiss and I'm a little nervous but follow his lead. My body tingles and I lean in closer wanting—no, needing—more and more. Enchanting turns to intoxicating the second his lips part and mine do the same. A wave of new sensations ripple along my skin, down my neck and spine like a runaway train. I want to die right here. Because right here, right now, I'm happier than I've ever been in my entire life.

When Dylan breaks the kiss—because I'm way too interested in indulging myself for as long as humanly possible—I try to catch my breath. My eyes open, close again on the next breath, then open finally to look up at his.

Enchanting changes to intoxicating and now that's changed to mesmerized. As I look into Dylan's eyes with my lips still tingling from his, I feel completely mesmerized by this mysterious new guy who came to our small supernatural town and set his sights on telepathic me.

I'm mesmerized and loving every minute of it.

I dream of Dylan.

We're on a beach, fluffy, peach-colored towels lined side by side as I lie on my stomach and he rises above to apply suntan lotion. The feel of his hands on me is incredible and he whispers periodically in my ear how pretty he thinks I am, how special.

Then I hear the noise, it's almost deafening. The brakes screech, iron against iron causing sparks to fly from the wheels. But it's too late, the train crashes and everyone is thrown from their seats. I'm floating. Again. Floating and feeling. It's dark this time and the nameless faces I saw before in various stages of death all blend together to form dark, smoke-face blobs. Until I float into the end cabin and see them sitting as they were, holding hands. This time Dad's not holding his stomach and Mom's forehead isn't bleeding. Yet, I still feel the pain in both locations. It's duller than before, almost numbing as if it's been there so long I've forgotten about it.

Her lips move, she's trying to talk, trying to tell me something. I can't hear her so I move closer. There's a warm breath coming from her lips but no sound. I pull back and look down at her with the intention of telling her I couldn't hear her when no sound comes out of my mouth, either. I'm speechless again.

Always.

I couldn't yell or scream for months after their deaths. And even now, a year later I'm not sure I did any of the above. Ever.

At the hospital I remember sitting in a waiting room full of people. I held my mom's purse and her book and what was left of Dad's laptop. It smells in the hospital, a scent that sticks with you if you spend more than five minutes in one. I hate inhaling because I know already I'll never forget. There are three televisions wired from the walls near the ceiling, all of them running the same show—an infomercial for acne medication. I only know this from the before-and-after pictures of people that once looked like something exploded on their faces and now look perky and clean. I can't hear the television. I can't hear anything.

Other than the screech of the train braking but not really stopping.

There's a lot going on. People moving all around. Some of them are from the accident. I can tell because their clothes are rumpled, splotched with blood and torn, just like mine.

I'm overwhelmed with sadness and pain unlike anything I've ever felt. My heart is breaking, literally and from the pain radiating from my chest on down, possibly physically. The paramedics said I was fine. They checked my vitals and touched all over me to make sure nothing was broken. I was not wounded in the crash.

Mom and Dad were killed.

I didn't need the doctors to come out and tell me this, but

they did, anyway. I don't recall reacting to their words, just sitting there staring ahead at all the activity that continued to go on, even though my parents were dead and my life would never be the same again.

The next thing I remember is the funeral, two caskets, two gravesites. One pitifully lonely evening in April of last year. In the morning, she was there. Aurora Hampton, my Guardian. She took my hand, this gruff-looking woman and looked me right in the eye.

"Everything happens for a reason," she said. "Never forget that."

Sitting up in my bed and rubbing my eyes I remember Mrs. Hampton's words. I remember the gray linen suit she wore and the worn, black-floral-print purse she carried. Her words linger in my mind as I think of the first time I saw Dylan.

It was in a dream, just like this one.

ten

Practice Makes Perfect

Dylan kisses me right in front of the girls' locker room. We'd walked from last period together toward the locker rooms since both of us had practice this afternoon. We didn't hold hands, just talked as we walked, about our day, boring classes, even more boring teachers. A simple conversation I guess I could have with any of the other students. But Dylan wasn't any other student. And that was an important difference.

"Meet you in the parking lot after practice," he says, his lips still close to mine.

I nod because words just don't seem ready to form in my head at the moment. Then he walks away, the boys' locker room is across the hall. With a sigh I push through the double doors and walk the small hallway before the two openings, the one to the left heading toward the coaches' offices and the one to the right to the lockers and showers.

My locker is near the end of the second row; it's the same locker I use for gym. I'm a little late so Davanna, Olivia and Keiley Mitchner are already at their lockers changing and chatting.

"Hi," I say when I get closer and start to twist the combination to open my lock. When it clicks open I throw my books and purse inside and grab my shorts and shirt.

I'm already pulling my T-shirt over my head when Olivia asks, "You and Dylan Murphy seem to be getting close, how long's that been going on?"

Generally speaking, my motto is that my business is my business. I think that comes from growing up in a political atmosphere. The last thing you want is everybody knowing every detail about your personal life, although sometimes it can't be helped. But in high school—in the girls' locker room, specifically—I know the rules are a little different. We're all on the cheerleading squad together, the norm is to share secrets, be each other's BFFs and giggle at just about anything the other said. It's a part of fitting in, something I assume I should do at some point, especially if I still want the "normal" life.

So I suck it up and reply, "We just started talking. He's really nice."

"You've been doing more than talking from what I just saw in the hall," Keiley says with a smile and a lift of her eyebrows.

Like I said, even if you don't offer your business on a platter to people, it seems they still find out.

My cheeks heat as I fold my jeans and throw them in the locker. "I guess it's getting serious." I don't really know but this is the kind of information they're looking for so I don't disappoint.

"He's seriously hot," Davanna adds. "And did you see that car he drives? I'd be his girl just for the chance to ride around in that baby."

This, for whatever reason, is extremely funny. The girls burst into those irritating little giggles—the ones I said were "normal," but still sound ridiculous.

"It is nice," I say because that's not a lie or an exaggeration. Dylan has a great car. I wonder what his parents do, how they can afford to give their son a car like that.

He hasn't talked about his family much. Not at all actually and of course I wonder why. Could be that he's from a political family like me and knows not to say too much too soon. Or could be something else, but I quickly dismiss that thought because being a Mysytx has made me question just about everything lately.

"Okay, so enough about the car," Keiley squeals, grabbing my arm and pulling me down on the bench beside her. "How does he kiss? He looks like he can really put one on a girl. Tell, tell, tell."

Is she serious?

Looking up at Olivia's and Davanna's equally curious and expectant gaze I presume she is and swallow hard.

"He's a great kisser," I say and feel my entire body blush at this point. Talking about this is definitely not normal, at least not for me.

A locker slams and the four of us jump and look to the other end of the aisle.

"Starting rumors, little foreign girl," one of the Langhorne twins says as they both ease into the aisle.

I said ease because they don't really walk, it's like they just appear somewhere, or slither, kind of like a snake.

Knowing instinctively this could be a touchy confrontation I stand and push my jeans into my locker. By the time I close and lock it one of the twins—the one that called me foreign—is standing right in front of me. The other one is on the other side of the bench glaring at me from behind.

I look right into her brown eyes and try for some kind of reading because it's obvious these girls do not like me, but I'm not a hundred percent sure why. I don't get anything.

"Rumors aren't usually true," is my only response and I move to push past her.

I don't really know why I thought it would be that simple. She pushes me back.

"He's not your boyfriend so you'd better stop telling people that."

It's not a statement but a warning; it doesn't take my empath skills to get that message loud and clear.

"I don't think that's any of your business," is my retort.

She laughs. "Oh, yes, it is my business. And I'm not going to tell you again to stop talking about him. Don't even think about him."

"That's right," the other twin chimes in. "Why don't you go and find one of your own kind?"

"Come on, girls, this isn't nice," Keiley speaks up from the other side of me. "We were only talking and he *did* kiss her and he *does* bring her to school and take her home. So it *does* look like they're going together," she adds in a tone that seems so normal.

I'm still reeling from the second twin's words about finding one of my own kind. I don't think she knows that could have two meanings—I could either find an Asian guy or a supernatural one. Either way I don't like her tone or her accusations, neither are necessary and I'm not tolerating them.

"Or you both can get your own boyfriends then you

wouldn't have to worry about who's mine or not," I say and this time when I push past the twin it's with enough force to slam her back into the locker out of my way.

I might be small and most always the outsider, but I learned early not to let people push me around. If I did they'd never stop. Besides, I'm not afraid of the twins, they're just mean girls and generally I don't give them too much attention. But as I walk out onto the field and the warm sun hits my face something else trickles through my mind. What if they're not just mean girls?

Practice ends two hours later with Ivy and Isis giving me the evil eye the entire time. By the time we go inside and get changed and I head for the parking lot, I'm so busy thinking about seeing Dylan again that I forget about them and the confrontation in the locker room.

Until I see them standing next to Dylan's car talking to Dylan.

It's not a big deal, I tell myself as I keep walking. For a second I think about turning around and running to catch the bus, then I stop. They're not running me away, I don't care how strange they are.

So I walk right up to them and touch Dylan's shoulder since his back has been to me the whole time. "Hey," I say with a smile.

When he turns he smiles back and everything Isis and Ivy said or did earlier melts away. "Hey. You ready?"

"Sure am. You girls getting a ride home, too?" I ask with the biggest, brightest smile I can muster.

Their faces are frozen in that mean glare they have. It's a shame because they're really pretty girls—too pretty, I think. They could have any guy in this school or in any school I'm sure, but I get the feeling they're both set on Dylan. Pity, I think with a small air of superiority that I'm feeling for the first time in my life. Wonder if this is "normal"?

"No. They have their own ride," Dylan says and takes my hand leading me around to the passenger-side door.

"Okay. Well, see you in practice tomorrow," I say to them just as I slip into the car.

When Dylan gets in and we pull off I think about asking him what they were talking about. He doesn't seem like he'd have much to say to them since their personalities are so different from his. Then again, they are very pretty, both of them.

But Dylan reaches over the console and takes my hand while he drives. I don't think about the mean twins again.

eleven

First Date

I don't know if I'm doing this right. The first-date thing, I mean. I had to sneak out of the house because telling Mrs. Hampton that I'm going on my first date is not going to go over too well—especially after my second run-in with that creature. I just know this without really knowing. I'm still not entirely over that so spending an evening with Dylan is the best thing for me right now. That way I don't have to think about the crazy thing chasing me or the fact that I think I've seen it before.

Maybe if my dreams weren't so vivid I wouldn't suspect everything is something I've seen before. But I dream in color. There's less than one percent of the population that does that. In addition to the color, in my dreams, there's scent and sound and most of all emotion. The train crash has become like this gruesome horror flick that just plays over and over again in the theater of my mind. I wish I could slip into another theater and watch something different just one night out of the week.

But what if it's trying to tell me something? What if

revisiting this dream over and over again is like a message and I'm too stupid to get it?

"You look great." Dylan's compliment breaks through my negative thoughts.

"Thanks," I say, sliding into the front seat of his car. The leather's cool against my bare legs since I picked a turquoise sundress to wear tonight. The air conditioner must be on high, a stark contrast to the stuffy humidity outside.

Music's playing softly on the radio but I can hear it's one of my favorites, "If I Die Young" by The Band Perry and I want to turn it up, but don't want to be too forward on our first date. When my seat belt is clasped I smile to myself because worrying that touching the radio is too forward is as lame as I can possibly get.

"I found this nice restaurant." Dylan's talking as he pulls off. "It's Chinese so you should like it."

The car gets quiet, like when somebody drops a book in the library and the room seems ten times as quiet as it was before.

"I'm not Chinese," I say slowly because I'm not sure if I should be offended or not. I mean, usually I know when someone's giving me crap about my Asian ethnicity, but I can't really tell what Dylan's purpose is just yet. Maybe by the end of tonight I'll feel better about the boy I saw in my dreams who appeared on my bus and is now taking me to dinner.

"My parents are from South Korea," I tell him so he'll know the next time to ask first instead of assuming. Okay, I guess I am offended.

Dylan nods. "My bad," he says and turns down the street that'll take us near the mall.

"But I like Chinese food," I offer since it's suddenly gotten quiet again. "What's your favorite food?"

He pauses then tosses me another one of those smiles. "What's yours?"

Okay, I'll accept that he's totally not trying to talk about himself. That's fine, for now.

"I have some favorite Korean dishes that my mom used to cook all the time. Kimchi is one and Dakkochi. Mmm, I miss her cooking so much," I say and my body fills with warmth. It's the memory, the taste and feel of it, that overwhelms me.

"What's that?"

"Kimchi is cabbage, garlic, onions and fish. It's in a light sauce and is absolutely fabulous when it's piping hot. Dakkochi is chicken on a skewer with spices that make your eyes water and your tongue burn."

"Sounds, ah, interesting," he says.

This is funny, not offensive. I guess it probably does sound strange to some people. If I told him half the customs and rituals we practice as South Koreans he'd probably say that was interesting, too. But I learned a long time ago that I can be proud of my heritage and not wear it on my sleeve at the same time. For instance, I have this beautiful south pearl bracelet that Mom gave me when I turned twelve. She told me that family is the most important part of Korean culture and this bracelet, that matched her earrings and the stone in Dad's favorite cufflinks, bonded this small portion of our family. I'll never forget that but I'm not telling Dylan, either.

"You said your mom used to cook it for you? She doesn't anymore?" he asks when we've traveled a little farther.

It's my turn to clear my throat. "No. She doesn't." I take a deep breath. "My parents were killed last year in a train crash." I don't see any harm telling him this part.

I wait to see if he has something to say about that, if somehow he'll remember being in my dream during the crash. I know it's crazy but I get the feeling there's something about Dylan that links us. Not like a love at first sight kind of link—even though I fantasize about that theory, as well. But, I don't know, I just think there's something…

"That's tough. So you living with family now?" he asks and his voice presses against something deep in my chest.

"I live with my guardian." She's not family but she's all I have. I don't say that. The conversation is already getting too serious.

When we get out of the car it's not at the mall, but down the street a little way. There are a couple of storefront shops that didn't want to pay the price for mall rental but still enjoy the benefits of getting lots of mall traffic. There's a restaurant on the corner called Panda Kitchen, it's Lincoln's version of P.F. Chang's. I presume this is where we're going.

The minute we walk inside I know it's not good. Not the food, but the aura I'm getting.

It's dark, red-papered walls with black tables. On each table is a square lantern with a dull gold light inside. A lady wearing tight black pants, a white blouse and enough shiny red lipstick to paint this entire building on her lips, walks toward us, menus in hand.

"Hello. Welcome to Panda Kitchen. Table for two?" she asks in her heavily Asian-accented voice.

Her eyes rest on mine and I know she's trying to figure out where I'm from and what to say to me. To some, we—Asians, I mean—look alike. But that's not true, there are distinct physical differences in Koreans, such as more pronounced jawlines, straighter noses and thicker lips. She's Korean, too, so I smile at her and say, *"Annyŏng hashimnikka."* It's a formal Korean greeting.

She smiles in return and with a nod leads us to a table near the back. Dylan takes his menu and waits while I open mine.

"You sure you don't mind being here?" he asks. "I don't want you to think I was being rude or anything. I just thought, you know." He shrugs.

"It's okay," I say hurriedly. It is okay, isn't it? I mean, I am different from the other students at Settleman's—as far as I can tell I'm the only Asian student there. But I've always been different, I'm used to that. I just thought here, with the group of friends I'd found, it would be easier. Anyway, I'm on my first date, I should be embracing the night, not over-examining every little thing.

"It's fine," I say and open my menu. I'm not really hungry now so I order shrimp fried rice with extra egg.

Dylan orders dumplings and beef broccoli. My temples start to throb and voices echo in my head. They're a low murmur at first, just snatches of conversation from around the room. I think because it's so dark my channels are sort of whacked. I can't hear the thoughts clearly but they're still coming to me, whispering to me. It's like a breeze blowing through my body, starting at the tip of my head and whisking downward.

"So how do you like living here? How do you manage being the new girl?" Dylan asks when the waitress has taken our orders and our menus.

I shake my head, trying to push the extra thoughts away. It doesn't really work but I swallow deeply and reach for the normalcy I crave.

"I like living here just fine." It's a lie. I hope he doesn't realize it. "How about you? Do you like it here so far?"

I look directly at him as I talk, wanting that connection two people get when their gazes are locked. That's when I see it.

Not his thoughts. I don't get any of those and I don't really know why. This has never happened before—but I'm not going to let that worry me. A night free of mind reading at least one person will be a welcome relief. Besides, I'm more concerned with what I see than what I can't hear right now.

For a brief second there's a flicker of something in his eyes. Shock. Confusion. Doubt. I don't know which but I know it was something.

"Why'd you have to move here?" I prompt, hoping he'll open up and I can explain what I've just seen.

Dylan just shrugs. Thick wisps of hair curl around his ears and I notice that dimple in his chin again. It's really prominent and I come to the conclusion that it's the finale to his otherwise gorgeous looks. It's almost eerie how picture-perfect he is.

"Guess it was just time for a change," is his reply. It's nonchalant and empty.

No knowledge is gained on my end. But then I'm thinking there's something else I should be paying attention to.

I don't know if dark is a feeling, but I can feel it now. My body goes still and my fingers tremble just a bit. There's darkness here, in the Panda Kitchen.

Dylan is talking, I see his mouth moving but I don't hear a word he's saying. My gaze is drawn to a corner table where someone sits alone. This someone is about Dylan's build, his face young, what I can see of it since he's wearing stunner shades covering half his face.

I know him. Or at least I think I do.

He's looking down at his hands, turning them over front and back, examining them as if he doesn't think they're real. His lips move like he's talking but there's no one there for him to talk to. A quick scan of the restaurant and all looks well. Nobody seems to notice this boy in the back talking to himself. Nobody but me.

And just when I think I'm losing my last little touch of sanity, the boy looks up.

I can't see his eyes but I feel them on me. His lips spread into a grin revealing level white teeth. That smile sends an itch of evil that swirls around my neck like fingers.

As I try to breathe my lungs feel tight, filled, clogged. I hiccup and hiccup and try to focus on the boy. I smell the smoke more than see it because now my eyes are blurring, watering with the effort of staying open. Lifting my palms I flatten them on the table and try to gather my strength.

He's here. Charon is here.

I'm alone. On my own. It's my turn now.

I've known this was coming, watched as he attacked each one of us individually. And now I'm up.

I get to my feet using my arm to cover my mouth and nose. Before I take a step I remember I'm not alone and look across the table to see Dylan. He's not there.

Or the smoke is getting so thick I can't see him. I can't really see much of anything right now. But I start to walk anyway, in the direction of the table where I saw the boy. I don't see him there. I don't see anything now.

I'm engulfed by the smoke, by the thick dark of it. My head is throbbing as a cool breeze scrapes over my skin. I hear voices, lots of voices and I want to scream because I don't understand any of them. They're all talking and talking, some trying to tell me something, others just hoping I'll hear. But I can't, the words are jumbled and the emotions are suffocated by the smoke.

I cough and cough until I feel like I'm going to spit out a lung. My entire body is shaking but I open my eyes anyway. Something inside urges me to open my eyes. And there he is.

The boy with the shades. He's laughing, his head falling back at what he thinks is hilarious. I cough on him, spit streaming from my mouth but he just keeps on laughing. Then I'm moving, not walking but drifting away. I can't see and can barely breathe but I hear my name being called.

"Lindsey? Lindsey?"

It's Dylan.

I try to say his name but it just comes out another cough.

"Calm down. It's all right, the paramedics are here."

I don't understand what he's saying. Paramedics? Where did they come from? Why did they come?

Dylan's cheeks are smudged with black, his hair disheveled.

"What—" I try to talk again around the coughing this time. "What happened?"

"Grease fire in the kitchen. You inhaled a lot of smoke," Dylan tells me before the paramedic pushes him to the side.

"We're taking her to the hospital. If you're not family I

suggest you call hers," the guy in the crisp blue-and-white jacket says to him.

Dylan nods. "Will do."

I lift my hand to him as he's drifting away. I don't want him to go and I don't want Mrs. Hampton to come. She's going to kill me for sneaking out.

"Stay," I manage to croak.

"I'll be right there," he says and the words are music to my ears.

At least momentarily.

The minute the doors to the ambulance close I hear something else. It's laughter, sick, ugly laughter that I know is coming from the boy in the glasses.

twelve

Caught

"YOU're safe now," I hear Dylan whispering to me.

They gave me something intravenously, something cold but oh so lovely. My throat still burns from all the coughing and my chest feels like a truck ran me over.

His hands are warm on mine but I want to touch his face. He won't let me move, holds my hands firmly as they rest on my stomach.

"Don't try to talk. They said you'll be hoarse for a couple of days."

"I want to go home," I say and wince at the raspy sound of my voice.

"Not a good listener, are you?" Dylan chuckles.

Then the door opens and in comes the cavalry.

"What happened to you?" Sasha asks, coming right up to the other side of my bed and clapping a palm on my forehead. "How'd you end up in a fire?"

At the foot of my bed Krystal and Jake appear.

"Thought you might need a friendly face," Krystal says and I know exactly what she means. Plus, I can read her thoughts clearly since I'm in this hideous white hospital gown and she's wearing a denim jacket over a tank top.

"Glad it was you," I say in response.

Krystal had a vision of me in the fire with Charon or with the boy in the shades. That's how they knew I was here since I didn't have my cell to call anyone.

"You okay?" Jake asks.

"She's not supposed to talk," Dylan says without turning to look at any of the others, just staring down at me.

"I'm fine," I say, curious as to where his change in tone is coming from.

"Well, we had to come and make sure," Sasha says, tossing Dylan a chilly glare. "We can't have you getting all banged up. What were they doing in that restaurant, burning pigs or cats on the grill? Two fires in two days, that's unreal."

It is. I know it and so do the others, that's another reason why they're here. But I don't want Sasha bringing that up right now.

Out of the corner of my eye I see Dylan frown. "It was just an accident," he tells them in a level tone. "I think we should leave and let her get some rest."

"That's what you think, huh?" Sasha asks, folding her arms over her chest and staring at him.

"She's been through a lot tonight," Dylan replies.

"Funny that she's been through so much when she was out with you," is Sasha's retort.

"I think he's right," Krystal intervenes with her normal peacekeeper self. An elbow to Jake has him nodding in agreement.

"Ah, yeah, we just wanted to see personally that you were all right. So we've seen, now we can go." Jake gives Sasha a look and she huffs like she normally does when she doesn't like what's going on.

"I don't want her to be alone," Sasha says.

"She won't be."

Mrs. Hampton walks into the room and it feels like a polar punch. Everybody is quiet, like pin-drop quiet.

"Hi," I whisper. "I'm okay." She's looking at me like I just gave the wrong answer to the Double Jeopardy question.

"Everyone go home. She will be fine now," she snaps.

Nobody wants to argue with Mrs. Hampton. Krystal waves, Jake nods and he's thinking we'll meet and talk about this later. Sasha gives me a warm smile.

"Sleep tight," she says then brushes my hair off my forehead again. She looks over to Dylan and her entire expression changes. "Sleep tight," she says again and her tone is almost as chilly as Mrs. Hampton's. Almost.

Dylan doesn't look at all fazed by her words. "I'll call you tomorrow."

He squeezes my hand and I squeeze his back. I'll be looking forward to his call.

When everyone files out of the room, Mrs. Hampton closes the door. She flicks off the overhead light then comes over to the bed touching the switch that brings a dull overhead light just above the bed. There's a large recliner chair that looks anything but comfortable beside the bed and she sits there.

For long minutes there's quiet, nothing but the sound of the machine aiding the IV that feeds into my arm, beeping. My eyes close and open, open and close. I think I should be sleepy because of the pain medication, but I'm not. And when Mrs. Hampton realizes that, she begins to talk in a low monotonous tone.

"We were selected by the great goddess to watch over you. The selection came even before your birth."

She's talking about the Guardians. I don't turn to look at her, just lie still and listen.

"I knew who you were the second you were born. Your parents did, too. She tells them, you know. As soon as they have the child she's chosen, she tells the parents. Sometimes one or both of them, it depends. It is an honor to be chosen."

"As a Guardian or a Mystyx?" I ask quietly.

"Both," is her quick reply. "To beat him you must all come together, bringing your power. That is the only way to banish him forever into the abyss of Hades. The Underworld is no longer strong enough to hold him."

"How?"

"At this point it is not so much a matter of 'how' but 'when.' The time has to be right and only Styx knows when that will be. He's trying to tap into your mind now, trying to confuse you so that you will not be ready. You must be very careful, Lindsey, not to let the thoughts or emotions get the best of you."

"How do I do that? I don't know how to control what I'm feeling or when I'm going to feel it. It all seems so overwhelming."

"You must not let it overwhelm you. This is your power, embrace it and make it do your will. Once you have done that he cannot touch you."

"What's with all these fires? Is that how he's attacking me?"

"He's looking for something that links you to death and to misery, those thoughts and emotions fuel this demon."

"The train crash," I whisper and see flashes of the train as we were taken out by the paramedics. There was fire and dark smoke, a broken machine that was powerful enough to carry hundreds from one destination to another, was destroyed. Just as Charon's ferry-carting souls to the Underworld had been destroyed by Styx.

"My parents are the link."

She doesn't respond and I know that it's true.

"Your guilt holds you hostage, Lindsey. Once you learn to let go you'll have the power to resist him."

Let go of my guilt? How do I do that? As long as I breathe and walk this Earth I'll remember that I survived a train crash that so many others did not, that my parents did not. It wasn't fair, they were so much better than me, so much more than I'll ever be.

Tears sting my eyes as Mrs. Hampton's words echo in my head. I don't know if I'm up for this challenge, if I can do what is required of me.

And if I'm not, where will that leave the Mystyx?

thirteen

Party Crasher

"What do you know about him, anyway?" Sasha asks
from her spot on her bed while she's picking out nail polish.

Sasha likes to be coordinated, all the time. So the blue
ruffled mini skirt and glittering silver tank she's decided
to wear to Trends must be accented by matching polish
and accessories. The plastic box of nail polish she's going
through seems endless but I have no doubt she'll come out
victorious.

We're in her bedroom surrounded by all things frilly and
girly, except for the glow-in-the-dark stars on her ceiling,
which are left over from her addiction to astronomy, so
she said. There are two double beds in Sasha's room which
remind me of the hotels we used to stay in when I traveled
with my parents. More often than not they were multibed-
room suites and the room designated to me always had two
double beds.

I'm on the other bed by myself, plumping up two pillows
that I can lie on. Krystal's standing near the book stand,
which holds more CDs and DVDs than actual books.

Since I already picked out my outfit for tonight and don't

really care if my black toenail polish matches it or not, I'm finished with all the primping I plan to do. Besides, we aren't leaving for another three hours. Krystal wants to watch a movie, but I know Sasha would want to talk, just as I know what she'd want to talk about. Damn these powers of mine.

"I know that he's cute and he likes me. That's enough for now," I say, hoping this will cut the conversation short. I should have known better.

"I didn't hear a word about him moving here. He just showed up and the minute he did, everyone at school started singing his praises. Don't you find that odd?" Sasha continues despite my inner warnings.

"Like Lindsey said, he's cute and he's on the football team, which by the way is winning like all their games. It's no wonder he's popular all around school." That's Krystal and I'm sending her happy vibes for being so supportive of me and Dylan.

Sasha drops a bottle of polish back into the box—I guess she didn't like that color.

"But he just showed up on your bus one day then starts picking you up and dropping you off the next," she quips. "I mean where did that come from?"

"You make it sound like I couldn't possibly catch the attention of a guy like that?" That sounds like I'm offended, and since I know how that feels now, I admit that I am.

"So not what I'm saying," Sasha huffs. "I'm just trying to figure him out."

Krystal comes over to the bed where I'm sitting and plops down on the end. She's holding ten DVDs and lets them all fall onto the bed beside her.

"Why? He's not dating you," she says, but doesn't look up at Sasha when she does. That's probably a good thing.

Another clinking of glass signals another bottle of polish that Sasha doesn't like. "I didn't say he was. But since we're friends we look out for each other. Right?"

We don't answer her. But it doesn't matter.

"So anyway, I'm just trying to look out for you. If he turns out to be the king of creeps, don't say you weren't forewarned."

Another crack of glass.

"You're going to make a mess," I say, looking over at her.

"Ugh!" she yells. "I'm just so stressed."

Now we get to the root of her problem. She is stressed and to my relief it's not about me or Dylan.

"About Twan," I say and it's not a question.

Sasha falls back on her pillows, her knees kicking the box of polish to the end of the bed. "He wants our relationship to go to the next stage."

Me and Krystal look at each other.

"Meaning the physical stage?" Krystal asks.

Sasha nods.

"I remember Franklin and I had that talk." Krystal groans. "Very stressful."

That was one of the first thoughts of Krystal that I read so I remember that, as well. Then it was easy for me to give advice. Now, since I have a boyfriend or a *boy friend,* too, I can't come up with a quick reply.

"What are you going to do?" I ask.

"I think I want to do it," she says quickly like she's afraid she'll forget if she doesn't get it out right away.

"Wow," Krystal says. "That's huge."

"What about you and Jake?" Sasha asks. "Are you two ready?"

Krystal quickly shakes her head. "Don't even want to think about that." She tosses down a DVD to solidify that announcement.

I chuckle. "I completely understand."

"So am I a slut for wanting to do it?" Sasha asks.

I shake my head. "No. It's a very natural urge. Just be careful," I warn.

Sasha looks over at me. "You, too, Linds," she says. "I mean that seriously. We don't know a lot about this Dylan guy and I'm not getting such a good vibe. That may not mean anything but I just want you to be careful, you know?"

I nod as I'm looking at her. "I know what you mean, and thanks for meaning it."

I know what she's trying to say and that she means it from her heart. I can't be mad about that. And since I've never had a friend really care about my best interests before, I grab hold of this moment and put it with the memories I'd most like to keep.

I expected the dark, am grateful for it, actually. Standing outside of Trends in a long line, I'm filled with a variety of emotions—hyperactivity, boredom, intrigue and anxiety being the most prevalent. I can't seem to shake that one and it's starting to make me nervous.

The thing about feeling everything others around you feel is trying to distinguish which emotion originates from yourself. I'm sure there's a way for me to differentiate but I clearly haven't mastered it yet. And according to Mrs.

Hampton, mastering my power is an absolute must for battling Charon.

I don't want to think about that tonight, don't want to go back two days to when my Guardian sat next to my hospital bed telling me how Charon is attacking me and what I need to do to stop him.

After standing in this line with people talking, thoughts shifting in and out of my head, I'm grateful to Twan for appearing.

"We're in. Let's go," he says, taking Sasha's hand.

Jake, Krystal and I follow to the front of the line and through the tinted glass doors marked Trends in swirling gold letters.

So there are four connecting large rooms that still seem filled to capacity. Everywhere I move I bump into someone and their emotions quickly spill over to me. By the time I get to the table in the third room that Twan leads us to I slouch down in the seat taking deep breaths.

"You all right?" Jake asks, touching a hand to my elbow.

I try to adjust myself in the seat so that I don't look like a drunk. "I'm fine," I say wistfully. But I'm not. My head hurts, is actually throbbing with the thumping beat of the music the sick DJ is playing.

Sasha and Twan immediately hit the dance floor while Jake and Krystal head to the bar to get something for everyone to drink. I tell Jake to bring me a cola, maybe the caffeine will counteract everything else that's going on inside me. After a few seconds I look at my watch, it's twenty after ten now and Dylan's not here. He said he'd meet us so I wonder if he's outside in the line. Pulling out my cell I send him a text then set it on the table to wait for a response.

While I'm waiting for Jake and Krystal to return or Dylan to text me back, I look out onto the dance floor where it seems hundreds of people are dancing to a hip-hop beat. A couple walks by the table and fear has me gasping. I mean literally I feel like I'm being choked and my hand goes to my throat. The guy is holding the girl's arm pretty tight and there's a stinging pain in my right arm as well. She's afraid of him, afraid of what he's going to do to her. I'm coughing by the time Jake and Krystal return.

"Here's your drink," he says, his eyes and body full of concern.

He knows something's wrong with me. I don't know how Jake and I communicate like this. It's just like a few months ago when he was grappling with his indecision. I could feel every wave of anger, every sensation of pleasure he experienced. At the cemetery I wanted to cry with the joy he felt at seeing his mother and the triumph that soared through him when he finally made the choice. Maybe it's because he's a Vortex, that's why he's so in tune to what's going on with me. I don't know but I gulp the cola down like it's literally saving my life.

"What time is Dylan supposed to get here?" Krystal asks. She's not looking at me but staring at the dance floor.

At least my mouth isn't cotton-dry anymore. I sit the now half-empty glass down and wipe my hand over my forehead. "He said he'd meet us at ten. I'm waiting for him to reply to my text now."

"Wow, Twan and Sasha really like dancing," Krystal comments as if she didn't even hear my answer about Dylan.

"Twan looks like he's enjoying himself," Jake adds with a grin.

I see them on the floor dancing. Twan's body is pressed tight against Sasha's. His hands are on her hips, his fingertips splayed so that they're touching her bottom. Sasha's hips gyrate in sync with Twan's. The music's kind of upbeat and yet they're stuck together like it's a slow song. Suddenly I'm hot. From my toes, which are out in the peep-toe Mary Janes I'm wearing, to my kneecaps which are bare in the miniskirt. My chest is even hot and I pick up my cola to finish it off.

"You think they're doing *it?*" I ask when my glass is empty. Mortification sweeps over me immediately because I can't believe those words just rolled out of my mouth.

"It sure looks like it," is Jake's reply.

Krystal shakes her head. "No. Sasha would have told us."

"Well, she wouldn't have told him," I add, nodding toward Jake.

"I'm glad for the small things in life," he quips and shifts uncomfortably in his seat. "Can we talk about something else?"

Krystal gives him a playful jab with her elbow and he leans over to kiss her lips. A sharp pang of jealousy shoots through me and instinctively I know that's my own personal feeling, not the remnants of someone in this club. Where's Dylan?

As soon as I think the question I see him weaving his way through the crowd. He's noticeable in this place because his skin's a lot fairer than anybody in here. Not just the black people, but even me. He just looks a lot paler today than he had before. Maybe we didn't get enough sun when we were at the pool or maybe because he's from up north, where they don't get intense heat or lots of sun. I don't know and am past caring when he slips into the seat beside me and smiles.

"Hey," he says in that deep voice that I've come to really like.

"Hey. I was worried. You were taking so long," I say, trying to speak over the music.

"Sorry," he says then leans in to kiss my lips.

Now I'm smiling, happy that I'm not the fifth wheel but a part of the couples' night. Everything seems right when Dylan is beside me. I'm not even bombarded with emotions like I was before, just the quiet pleasure at being near him.

Sasha and Twan are back at the table now and Twan immediately speaks to Dylan.

"I see you made it. I was going to go out to see if you had problems in the line. I gave them your name and told them to let you in," he was saying after he and Dylan shook hands and Twan and Sasha sat down.

"Yeah, and Lindsey was concerned," Krystal says, looking at Dylan closely.

"I just got caught up, that's all. But I'm here now," he says and looks a little agitated.

Yes, he is here now, that's all that matters to me, I think to myself as he slips his arm around me and pulls me close. My eyes cut over to Sasha, who's lifting the glass Jake brought her to her lips and taking a sip. Her gaze is locked on Dylan and I'm hoping she keeps her mouth shut about her opinions.

"The music is great, isn't it?" I ask to steer our conversation in another direction.

Twan nods quickly. "I told you this DJ was the truth."

"He's good." Jake nods.

"You guys gonna dance?" Sasha asks. "Me and Twan are going back out."

She's already standing and she looks right at Dylan when she says, "Come on, Dylan, don't be shy. Show us what you've got."

I want to pinch her or shake her or something for singling him out. Instead, I stand up and take Dylan's hand. "We'd love to," I say, knowing full well I'm not a dancer.

If someone asked me to do a front tumble with two off-the-floor twists that would be no problem. Dancing and keeping this rhythm is going to be a challenge but I'm game since we're here.

Soon all three couples are on the dance floor and it becomes more fun than effort. I don't have any idea what I look like but I'm feeling the music and moving accordingly. Dylan seems to be enjoying himself, too, and for now that's all I'm concerned with.

It's not long before the song changes. At first I think it's another club tune with a few lines of hip-hop thrown in here and there. Everybody on the dance floor seems to move to the same rhythm as they had before. But I hear something else. It's faint, this sound, like a voice that starts off really slow. I can hardly understand what it's saying but I hear it and believe it's speaking to me.

It says my name and I turn to see if someone's behind me.

"Hey, I'm over here," Dylan says, touching my arm. I turn back to look at him.

He's smiling at me, his blue eyes sparkling. I smile back

and try to push whatever's going on in my head out of the way. It's about here and now, Dylan and I dancing and having fun.

There's a multicolored light that travels around the room making us all look like we're in some psychedelic funnel cloud. Reds and blues, greens and yellows, a rainbow of colors that flickers in my peripheral.

Dylan reaches for my hands, pulls me closer. He's grinding against me and I like it. My entire body flushes with the contact as he leans forward and kisses my cheek, my chin, my neck. My legs are getting wobbly, which is not going to help my already suspect dance skills.

Then someone grabs my arm. I feel like I've been doused with cold water and spin around to hurl some not-too-pleasant words at the person interrupting.

But it's Sasha and she looks funny.

Krystal's right beside her giving me a serious frown. "Ladies' room. Now!"

I don't have time to mutter anything but, "Sorry," to Dylan who looks not puzzled but kind of irritated as I'm being pulled away from him.

"What's going on?" I ask the minute we enter the ladies' room. "What's wrong with you?"

Sasha's bending over the sink turning on the water and splashing it onto her face.

"She saw something," Krystal says.

It's not exactly what she just said but how she said it, in a low kind of whisper, that tells me whatever Sasha saw was not normal. I grab some towels and hand them to Sasha, who is a little pale and is breathing heavy.

"What'd you see?"

"It was hideous," she starts as she drags the towels over her face. "Fangs and bright green eyes. Clawed fingers and big, bigger than anything I'd ever seen."

"In here?" I'm asking because the club may have ten-foot ceilings at best. How big could something be without crowding out the other occupants or causing a scene?

"On the dance floor with us. I saw it reaching for…" She pauses, looks at Krystal then at me. "Reaching for you."

Me? I don't ask that because I hate the echoing effect. I heard her and she's looking right at me so there's no question who she's talking about.

"Then I'm glad he didn't get me," I try to joke but it sounds sickly.

This bathroom is clean as far as public bathrooms go. It has black doors on all the stalls and a muted kind of green color on the walls. The sinks are unclogged and clean and there aren't any wet towels on the floor. There's a mirror across the entire back of the sink and I sneak a look at my face and almost groan. I look afraid even though I'm trying not to be. Krystal's afraid, thick waves of fear roll off her and my body absorbs them like a super-soaker sponge. Sasha's pissed and nervous. She's looking at me like she expects an answer or a response. I don't have either.

"It was standing right next to Dylan but it wasn't reaching for him," she says suddenly.

I jerk back because the words are accusatory and feel like a slap. I'm already shaking my head. "Nothing touched him. We just danced but nothing touched him." I would have known, would have felt the evil coming, getting near him. Dylan isn't like us so me being with him is a threat. I have to keep that in mind when I'm with him.

Sasha and Krystal are both silent.

"It was just a sighting," I continue. "You've been seeing magicals for a while now. Too bad you aren't used to it yet."

"I'm not used to seeing them right next to my friend's boyfriend reaching to rip her throat out," Sasha says adamantly.

"Don't be dramatic, Sasha. If it was reaching for me you and Krystal got me out of there in time. So let's just calm down and go back out to enjoy ourselves."

I don't want to stay in here and talk about this anymore. I don't want to think about what was near Dylan or why it was near Dylan or why it was reaching for me. I just don't want to go there, not tonight.

Clearly, that's not the plan.

There's a loud boom and then we hear screaming. Without another word we run to the door and out into a chaotic crowd. There's more screaming and people seem to be scattering everywhere. I'm heading toward the room where we left Dylan, Twan and Jake on the dance floor. Krystal's right behind me.

There's another thud and the building seems to shake. My throat gets tight as the lights flash on and off and I'm thrust back into a time when the lights flashed and everything around me moved. I'm feeling a lot now, throbbing in my temples, heart pumping wildly. I'm panting like I've been running for miles, probably a combination of everyone running to get out of here.

I bump into Jake, who's heading in our direction. "We gotta go now!" he says, reaching past me to grab Krystal's hand.

Twan is right behind him and Sasha squeezes past me to get to his side.

"What happened?" she asks.

"Something's here," Jake says and starts pushing in the opposite direction to guide us out.

I don't want to leave. "Where's Dylan?" I ask.

"He was right behind us," Twan answers without looking back at me.

I look back, stand on tiptoe and avoid being knocked to the floor as I wait for Dylan. If whatever Sasha saw was standing near Dylan I need to make sure he's okay. Sickness pools in the center of my stomach as I think of Dylan being hurt because of me.

Sasha looks back for me, she's telling me to come on, but I don't move. And I can't talk. Jake was right, there's something here. I feel it. Something evil and angry is here and it's hungry. My eyes continue to scan the crowd looking for Dylan but I still don't see him.

There's another loud boom then all the lights go out. Windows shatter, glass hitting the floor in a sick crackling sound. People are screaming louder. But not me. I cannot scream. I stand still, closing my eyes to the fear rippling through me. I don't know if it's all mine or from others around me. There's so much screaming and it seems to go on and on. I think my head's going to split right open.

Along my spine a tingling sensation moves, traveling like fingers, climbing, climbing, reaching for my neck and when it gets there, the grip tightens. My eyes shoot open instantly only to see it's still dark. I'm panting now wanting desperately to join in the other screams, to call out for Jake or Krystal or somebody to help me but I can't. Then I hear my name. It's a loud scream in a female voice. The same voice I heard earlier.

A door slams closed and it sounds close; my skirt and hair lift and toss in the cool breeze blowing throughout the room now. My name's being called again. I can't see anyone, don't know where to go or what to do. Then there's another loud thump and I'm airborne. I don't feel anything but gravity pulling me along some path I can't distinguish. I land with a thump and a hand touches my arm instantly.

"Lindsey!"

It's Krystal, she's right beside me pulling me until I'm upright. "Are you okay?"

I still can't speak but I nod my head. We're outside now, it looks like in the back alley but I should have broken every bone in my body being thrown out the window like I believe I was. There's a gruesome roar and both of us look up to see a creature at the end of the alley. It's huge and black with sharp fangs that drip with some cloudy mucus that burns a hole right through the sidewalk when it hits.

"Oh, my god!" Krystal says, grabbing hold of my arm.

Jake steps in front of us, pushing us back. "Stay behind me."

"Where's Sasha?" Krystal asks.

"I'm here," Sasha says, running up behind us. "That's it. That's what I saw in the club." She points at the creature.

"That looks wicked bad," Twan says, coming to stand beside Jake.

He's right, it does look bad. And all of us can see it, not just Sasha.

"What do we do?" Twan asks like he's one of us.

The creature takes a step toward us and Jake pushes us back. "Run!" he yells and we all turn around and do just that.

Tires screech along the asphalt as people drive cars in a

frenzy to get away. There's more screaming as we scramble around heading for the parking lot ourselves. You would think since we're the powerful ones we would stand and fight, but I don't have a clue what this thing is or what it wants and I doubt the others do, either. Besides, Jake has the only active power. And just as I think about it, he turns and looks at two pickup trucks, sending them hurling through the air to land in front of the creature, halting his step. But the diversion is only a momentary one. The creature lifts its larger-than-life feet and stomps right down on the truck like it was a Tonka and not a Toyota.

Fury rips through my body, halting my steps, bending me forward with a fierce pain in my stomach.

"Lindsey! Let's go!" Krystal's yelling from behind me but I can't move.

I can't think. In my mind I feel like I've been in this predicament before. The last outcome was devastating. My body and mind both pray this doesn't end the same.

Jake grabs my arm and shakes me. "What's wrong with you? We've got to get out of here."

I know his words are true but I can't move. I can't speak. I can't do anything but watch what happens. Like I watched my parents die. Like I watched that thing from the water. Like I'm watching this creature walk toward me now.

With its arms outstretched, it's mashing the buildings on the street that are tall enough. It opens its mouth and gives a deafening roar that sends infernally hot air whipping around.

Jake finally lifts me up and carries me to the car. All the females are in the backseat of Sasha's car. Jake pushes the seat down and climbs into the passenger seat while Twan runs around the car to get into the driver's seat. But before Twan can make it inside, the creature lunges forward extending its arm toward the car.

Everything goes into slow motion then. Each movement of the creature is like in freeze frame. Krystal's and Sasha's screams are extended, echoing throughout the car. I see the creature's clawed hand open. Twan lets out a fearful cry about a second before his body is scooped up by the creature's hand.

Beside me Sasha's screaming stops as she sucks in a breath. Coming forward she grabs the headrest of the driver's seat and calls Twan's name. Krystal grips my hand and Jake jumps out of the car. But he's too late. With a flick of the creature's gigantic hand, Twan's body flies through the air landing with a gruesome thunk on a rooftop to one of the nearby buildings.

"No!" Sasha yells, her entire body shaking with the effort. Krystal's chanting, "Oh, my god! Oh, my god! Oh, my god!"

I'm silent. Completely.

My eyes blink and blink like that sole action will change what I've just seen. Then there's Dylan, running across the street, away from the creature. I want to call out to him but I can't.

Outside the car Jake's moving everything aside, tossing cars and lampposts—anything within range at the creature, which just continues to roar in response. Finally Jake looks down at the ground, his fists balled at his sides and lets out a roar of his own. With that sound and his gaze fixed on the concrete, the ground rumbles and splits, creating a path that runs right into the creature. When it takes another step that huge claw foot falls into the widening crack and it stumbles. Putting his hands together then spreading them wide, Jake increases the opening in the ground until the creature falls completely inside. Everything around us shakes. Jake slaps his hands back together and the crack in the ground closes with sparks of fire and thick black smoke emanating into the air.

The creature is gone.

Sasha's crying uncontrollably.

Krystal's trying to console her but she's crying, as well.

I finally open my mouth and the tiniest whisper escapes, "He came for me."

fourteen

Grief

MY chest hitches each time Sasha takes a breath. When she exhales, warm tears stream down her face. My eyes are swollen with the effort. We sit on Sasha's bed, the three of us—me, Sasha and Krystal—linked by arms and sorrow.

Twan is dead.

There's nothing more definite than death. And at this moment, nothing more painful. You'd think I'd be good at this by now, but grief is the worst emotion ever invented. Give me fear, or pain any day because grief is a hideous evil.

Sasha wonders why Twan had to die. I'm wondering the same thing. Why was he singled out? If the creature came for me he could have just as easily plucked me up and tossed me around. But it hadn't and I'm beginning to feel really sick about that.

"I should call his grandmother," Sasha says between sniffles and hiccups.

She's been doing that, talking sporadically between her tears. It's all about Twan, about his life and what he was going to do with it. Her heart's broken and I don't know how to fix it.

"The police are probably doing that," Krystal says in a quiet voice.

Once Jake had finally gotten into the car he'd pulled off so fast all I'd seen were the flashing blue-and-red lights of the arriving police cars. In the backseat with me, Krystal had held Sasha, who was crying hysterically. We'd come straight to Sasha's house, not just because we were supposed to be sleeping over anyway but because this was the one house where we didn't have to worry about parental or adult supervision. Nobody here would ask what had happened, which is kind of sad and kind of good at the same time.

Mouse had opened the door for us, his face a mask of gloom. He knew what had happened, I could tell by the way he simply moved to the side and let us come in. When we'd walked up the steps with Sasha he hadn't said a word. At the top of the steps I turned back to look at him and he'd closed the door, was standing at the bottom of the steps, arms folded over his chest watching us. He was planning, I could sense it.

"She won't understand," Sasha says. "Nobody's going to understand."

I don't say anything because she's right. The police are going to be trying to figure out how Twan got up on that roof and if any witnesses were left in the parking lot, they're probably going to tell the police we were the ones with Twan. We should have stayed there. Should have waited and answered the questions right then. Jake cursed all during the ride back to Sasha's house. His fingers gripped the steering wheel so hard I thought he was going to rip it right out. We didn't know what to do right then. None of us did. We don't know what to do now.

"He wasn't even one of us," she sobs, pulling up her knees and burying her face in the pillow she held there.

A tear rolls down my cheek and I finally find the voice to speak again. "It doesn't matter," I whisper. "It's an all-out war now. They're not going to come for just us because they're not sure they can beat us. But they're showing us what they're capable of."

"They're testing us again," Krystal adds.

We look at each other over Sasha's bended body. Krystal thinks it's time for us to put an end to this madness. I agree. Sasha's in no mood to think or talk about this now. With silent concession we both acknowledge that.

I help Sasha up and into her nightgown while Krystal goes into the bathroom and grabs a warm cloth. We pull back the comforter and help her ease beneath it. Then, because she's our friend and our hearts are as heavy as hers after tonight's events, we climb into bed beside her. Krystal uses the warm cloth to wipe Sasha's face. I pull the covers up over her and then we lie back. The three of us, the Mystyx, minus one. Jake just left us here then sped off. None of us knew where he was going, even though I suspected. He'd return back to the scene to see what the police had to say. He'd want to see Twan again because they were close and Jake—he'd want to grieve alone.

Sometime in the middle of the night I hear a cell phone vibrating. Climbing out of the bed I stumble, remembering I'm not in my own room. Finding my purse I grab my phone, seeing the light on the screen blaring so I know it's mine that's going off.

"Hello?" I whisper because the last thing I want is to wake Sasha. It took forever for her to calm down enough to sleep. I'd like her to stay that way for a while.

"Hey."

His voice is a welcome relief. I remember seeing Dylan running toward the car after the creature attacked Twan. I wanted to call out to him, to tell him to come with us quickly but I couldn't. Then I didn't see him again. And with everything else that happened I didn't try to find him.

"Where are you?" I ask, still whispering and moving toward the door at the same time.

"I'm right outside. Come on down."

He's outside, of Sasha's house?

"I'm not at home," I say, pulling the bedroom door closed behind me.

"I know. You're staying at Sasha's tonight. I'm in front of her house."

I stop right at the top of the stairs at his words. How does Dylan know where Sasha lives? "Okay," I say slowly, disconnecting the call before he can say another word.

It's dark out here in the hallway but as I walk down the steps I get the feeling I'm not alone. Somewhere in this darkness Mouse is lurking. I know this and can't decide if that's comforting or just weird.

Because I know he's watching I don't even try to tiptoe or be any quieter than I am. I just head for the front door and pull it open wide enough to slip out. Sasha's house has an alarm, one that didn't go off when I open the door. Another dead giveaway that Mouse is watching me.

Dylan is right there as soon as I come out the door. He holds out a hand but I'm hesitant to take it.

"How did you know where Sasha lived?" I ask this first because it's one of many questions I want to ask him.

I don't know why all my questions have waited until this second to burst into my mind but suddenly there are a lot of things I want to ask Dylan Murphy.

His answer is only a shrug of his shoulders. "Walk with me," he says.

Why is this not as exciting an offer as it should be? Tonight's been an eventful night. Actually, I've had a couple of pretty eventful days. I'd like nothing more than to sit and talk to the boy I consider somewhat my boyfriend and feel some sort of comfort. But something tells me that's not going to happen.

Regardless, I walk with him. But I don't take his hand. "What happened to you at the club?"

"I went to the bathroom and when I came back everyone was gone."

When he said this I stop and just stare at him. "You didn't hear all that noise?"

"I heard some screaming—that's why I came out running. I couldn't find you." He stops at the end of Sasha's driveway and takes my hands in his.

I look into his eyes, they seem to be darker blue now, maybe because it's night. But as I look into Dylan's eyes this time I notice something. I think I've noticed before but it's really hitting me now. I can't read his thoughts.

I continue staring, keep trying to focus on his mind and what might be going through it. Nothing.

"Why are you looking at me like that?" he asks.

It's my turn to shrug because I don't really know how to say, "Ah, I'm trying to read your mind," without sounding like a complete idiot.

"I saw you getting in the car and I called to you but I guess you didn't hear me," he continues. He's rubbing his thumbs over the backs of my hands now and it's sending little slithers of heat down my spine.

I have on pajama pants and a tank top and there's a slight breeze out tonight. My feet are in flip-flops and my hair's up in a ponytail. All this equates to not being at my best but the way he's looking at me, it's obviously not my worst, either.

He was running toward the car, I saw him. He looked like he was in one of those commercials where they have bare-chested guys running along the beach, wind blowing through their hair leaving you breathless just watching. Even with everything going on around him, that's what I remember he looked like, except he had his shirt on.

Another thing I remember that startles me a bit is that he was running casually. Not like someone with a freaky large creature right behind him. Maybe the creature wasn't visible to everyone. Maybe just the Mystyx saw it?

But Twan saw it? Didn't he?

"Did you see anything strange?" With everything that's happened this week I'm wondering if the entire town of Lincoln is about to record extraterrestrial sightings. Which, coincidentally, would not be a good thing right now. So far the fire at the school was only reported as a fire—nothing out of the ordinary. But tonight seemed different. Maybe it was just different in my mind.

"The club's a mess, Everybody bailed for some reason but

I'm not sure why. There were cops out front when I came out."

And a large creature that looked like someone had ripped him right out of the pages of a Greek mythology textbook. But he hadn't said that. And he's not thinking it so I can't tell if he saw it or not. I guess it wouldn't be strange if he didn't, not any more strange that I did. My temples throb with the thought.

I don't know what to do or say around Dylan at this moment. Do I tell him that one of my best friends just finished crying her eyes out because her boyfriend died? Or do I just stand out here and act like it's all cool that I'm at a sleepover and this really cute guy snuck out in the middle of the night to see me?

"I was really worried when you just pulled off. I wanted to make sure you were safe," he says and something flashes in his eyes.

It's just a spark but I see it and I want to hold on to it because it feels true.

"I'm fine. I was, ah, a little upset when we were leaving. Sorry I didn't answer you," I say because maybe he didn't see anything out of the way. Maybe this was just another incident for the Mystyx to deal with. Except this time a human had been killed.

"I'm glad you're okay."

He steps closer to me and I don't know if he means to kiss me or not but I put my head down, let my forehead touch his shoulder. Dylan wraps his arms around me then, just folds me right into his embrace and I go willingly. My arms twine around his neck and hold him close. I feel like crying and screaming at the same time. I want to know why

Twan had to die, why Charon is fighting so dirty and why I keep choking up every time danger shows its ugly head.

I'm not getting those answers right now, which is kind of okay, since what I am getting is something else I've always wanted.

There's this guy standing here with his arms around me and he wanted to make sure I was okay. For the first time since I originally met grief, I feel like there's something to combat the hideous feeling. And that something's name is Dylan.

fifteen

The Morning After

when I wake up it's to the sound of drawers opening and closing and the television blaring. I roll over until I'm on my back, dropping an arm over my forehead. The assumption is it's morning because my eyelids twitch and dread opening to the light. And because that's what the newscaster just announces.

"Four dead in Arkansas as floods and tornadoes strike again," the newscaster continues saying.

My eyes open slowly and I peek at the television. This isn't the same meteorologist that was on last week. Actually, there's been a different one just about every week since Walter Bryant went on hiatus—the network's words, not mine. We believe Walter Bryant skipped town with Sasha's dad to further pursue the mysterious Project S. I wish we could have uncovered more about that project but right now I think our biggest concern is what's here in Lincoln. Oh, and what seems to be spreading across the nation like a sick disease.

"In Missouri, a warning of imminent failure for a levee on the Black River in the southeast part of the state prompted the mandatory evacuation of about a thousand people." Her name is Lily Barton and as I suspected she's new in town and new to the local news. She's pretty enough with her heavy auburn curls and wide model-like smile. Unfortunately, what she's saying isn't as attractive.

"In Vilonia, Arkansas, a town of three thousand people north of Little Rock, one death and between fifty to eighty houses were destroyed by a tornado, according to Faulkner County emergency management. Emergency workers report a path of destruction half a mile wide."

"Jake just texted me," Krystal interrupts and my gaze shifts from the television to where she sits on the edge of the bed. She's still wearing her nightshirt, her hair's all wispy around her head and she's holding her cell phone.

I hear another drawer slam and both of us look to the other side of the room where Sasha stands holding a top in each hand. "Blue or green? Which matches these shorts better?" she asks.

I guess the first thing I notice about Sasha this morning is how pretty she is. She's Colombian and has the warmest, brownest eyes I've seen. Her hair is simply gorgeous, long, shiny, healthy. Her body is going to be killer when she hits adulthood full-on and she has this cool friendly personality that just pulls you right in to her world whether you want to be there or not. She's honest and she's loyal and she's a friend of mine. I still want to pinch myself on that note.

She's looking at us expectantly as I pull myself up to a sitting position, my arms and legs aching like I've been in a full-body collision instead of asleep in this big bed most of the night.

"Green," Krystal says, then follows up with, "Jake wants to meet in an hour. He's coming over."

Sasha throws down the blue shirt, pulling the green one over her head. She's wearing cut-off jean shorts and her feet are bare, neon-pink toenail polish waving like a happy flag. She scoops her hair out of the shirt and lets it fall down her back as she turns to face the mirror. "Right, green," she says, turning sideways then to the back, then back to full-frontal mirror view.

Krystal and I look at each other and shrug. I'm used to dealing with my own grief, not necessarily someone else's. I think Krystal might actually be better at this since she's used to dealing with the dead all the time. Although Sasha's not the one dead.

"That'll look great for when we meet with Jake," Krystal says, getting up off the bed. "You should probably tell Mouse what happened last night. If they're attacking out in the open now, none of us are safe. The more we have looking out for us on this end, the better."

Sasha spins around, her hair following her in a silky halo around her face. "I was thinking we could see a movie today."

With a heavy heart I recognize exactly what Sasha's doing. "The first stage of grief is denial," I say kind of quietly and know that only Krystal hears me. Sasha is hearing nothing but her own words right now.

I'm slipping off the bed as Krystal takes Sasha by the shoulders. "You look great," she says first and Sasha smiles.

It's a wobbly smile faltered only by the clouding of her eyes, the pooling of tears about to fall. "And it's not your fault," Krystal continues. "It's not any of our fault. What happened just happened. And—" Krystal hesitates and takes a deep breath.

"Twan doesn't blame you."

Oh, crap, that's right, Krystal can talk to the dead.

Tears spill from Sasha's eyes and her whole body crumbles to the floor. Krystal goes down with her and I cross the room falling to my knees beside them. Sasha lays her head on Krystal's shoulder and I rub her back. The crying is intense, gut-wrenching and contagious. I'm crying. Krystal's crying.

Outside the wind is howling, like it, too, is having a hard time dealing with this loss.

An hour and a half and a whole pot of coffee later we're sitting in Sasha's family room. Sasha is in a chair surrounded by colorful pillows, which makes her look even sadder than she had lying on her bedroom floor.

Krystal sits on the couch not far away from Sasha. I sit on the other end of the couch and Jake has pulled up a chair from the small table in the corner where an unplayed chess game always sits.

"It's been all over the news for weeks now, all these tornadoes. It's like they're swarming the country or something. People are dying," Krystal says, then pauses and sneaks a look at Sasha who is pulling the fringes on one of the pillows. "There's mass destruction and they just keep coming."

Jake nods. "I know. I've seen the reports. The really strange thing is they aren't even trying to explain it. Like normally they'd said 'oh, it's global warming' or 'it's El Niño,' now they're just saying 'another tornado touches down.' It's like a weird kind of normal."

"Not weird," I add, rubbing my fingers along the hem of my black jean capris. "Maybe a prelude."

"A prelude to what?" Krystal asks.

"The beginning of the end," Jake says slowly. "Remember the symbols on the tree trunk? I think that was our warning. Sasha said she was led to that spot, to that tree. We all felt the energy there. We were supposed to go there, to get that message."

I'm nodding because what he's saying clicks into place. I'd already researched this, just never had the chance to tell everyone what I came up with.

"On the scroll you found in your yard it said the same thing. The Alpha and Omega, they are the beginning and the end of the Greek alphabet."

"What else did it say?" Jake asks.

"It's a prophecy of the beginning—good and evil where they're always combating each other. In the end one will be left standing, only one will prevail to rule the universe." I remember the words, the intricately written Greek letters. That message had been for Jake. The one in the forest for Sasha. Krystal's came from the spirits. And mine, it seemed the creature was bringing my messages right to my front door.

"He's trying to tell me something," I say, looking out the window. "He wants me to know that he's here and he's capable of bringing death. Just like he did on the train with my parents."

"Who?"

"This creature that Charon has sent as a messenger," I answer, not realizing I've had this answer for a couple of days now. But as I speak it just clicks right into place.

"He can't fight in this realm, not for himself. He's using

a demon that can roam this realm freely. The Darkness," Jake adds.

"His name is Lor," Mouse's deep voice echoes from the doorway. And as he walks with heavy steps into the room he continues to speak in that monotone accent. "He is a beastly demon from the Underworld whose real form was once too hideous to be seen in this realm. The fact that you have seen him, all of you, is not a good thing. It means that evil is gaining momentum. Charon is growing stronger."

"It means we're losing this fight," Jake says with a sigh, sitting back in his chair.

Mouse has been moving about the room, closing all the blinds and pulling heavy drapes over them. Just as Mrs. Hampton had done that night at our house. "Not exactly."

"Then what does it mean?" Krystal asks.

"I cannot tell you how to fight this fight," Mouse says when he comes to stand by the chair where Sasha sits not looking at anyone. "I can only tell you that it will take all of your combined strengths and powers at the precise moment in time. It will mark Charon's end."

"And in the meantime," I say because Mouse hasn't really told us anything we don't already know, "we sit back and watch innocent people die? That doesn't make sense."

"She's right," Jake adds. "It seems like we should be doing more to protect the ones who don't have power."

"You are coming into your full power," a familiar female voice says. "Each of you will need your full power during this time."

"Fatima," Sasha whispers as she looks across the room to the white-robed messenger she met in the Majestic.

When Sasha stands, Fatima reaches out a hand. It's a

little surreal to see Sasha go to this shimmering shadow of a woman and actually embrace her.

"Your pain is great and not unexpected, but it will make you weak." Fatima speaks with her arms around Sasha but she's looking directly at me. "And Charon preys on weakness."

"Yeah," Jake says, nodding his head. "He does."

Charon had attacked Jake when his grandfather died.

"So what do we do now?" Krystal asks. "How do we keep innocent people safe and prepare for this fight at the same time?"

Fatima releases Sasha and looks over at Mouse, whose arms are folded over his massive chest. "You cleanse your mind, strengthen your hearts and let your power guide you. Answers will not always be in front of you, but they will come to those who hold the power to reveal them."

Jake frowns and I know—even without reading his mind—that he's not liking Fatima's cryptic message. I, on the other hand, get exactly what she's saying.

sixteen

No Introduction Necessary

school is quiet and dreary, even for a Monday morning. Over the weekend everybody heard about what happened to Twan. As far as I can tell the police have reported it as an accident, but there're whispers of suicide.

Sasha visited with Twan's grandmother yesterday. Her mother went with her. When I called her last night she said that things went "fine." She's not real big on lengthy explanations right now and she's not in school today.

At lunch Jake went to the library so Krystal and I sat at our table, just the two of us. I saw Dylan this morning in class but haven't seen him since. I'm so confused on what we're doing together but more concerned about the state of the world if we can't stop Charon or at least head off his next attack.

"Who are they?" Krystal's question snaps me out of my thoughts.

I turn to stare in the direction she's looking and sigh. "Just two new girls. Twins I think, Isis and Ivy something or other. They're on the cheerleading team with me."

"Oh. More newcomers to Lincoln," she says and I look

at her. She thinks it's strange that we've had so many new arrivals in the past year. I've thought that, too, so I don't say anything. No use being repetitive.

"They're very pretty," Krystal notes.

I've already seen them, there's no need to look back again. Besides, there's more action on the other side of the cafeteria where one of the guys Twan used to hang with is arguing with a jock. Their anger is intense, fueled by the burn of grief and the indignation of embarrassment.

Trigga, his real name's Braxton Lewis, is tall and stocky with mean eyes but a quick smile. He and Fats, the shorter, rounder one who is now standing right by Trigga's side with an awesome grimace on his face, used to be like Twan's shadows. At least until he started going out with Sasha. Both the guys liked Sasha and didn't give Twan too much grief about being with a richie. It was like they were this ethnically blended family. Now Twan was gone and Sasha wasn't here. Trigga and Fats looked more than a little lost right now.

Pierce Haynes, the captain of the football team, is standing with Dylan. I try not to gasp in shock because Dylan is on the team. It stands to reason he and Pierce would hang out together. Only it looks like Dylan's all for a fight with Fats and Trigga, as well. Before I can explain to Krystal I'm up and moving toward the altercation.

A lot of other kids are, too, nothing more exciting on a dreary Monday than a fight in the cafeteria. As I get closer I can hear the argument.

"He was probably high on something and thought he could fly," Pierce chuckles as if he's a famous stand-up comic. "Dude, you're not Superman," he continues, holding his stomach like he's laughing so hard it hurts.

"Shut your mouth," Trigga said, stepping closer to Pierce.

Pierce sobers. "And if I don't?" He steps right back at Trigga.

"I'll shut it for you."

There's a lot of cheering on both sides. "Do it," Pierce dares.

And Trigga swings, his beefy fist connects with a loud crack against Pierce's jaw. The next blows come too fast and fiercely for me to accurately commentate. But I'm hustling through the crowd trying desperately to get to Trigga, to pull him away before Principal Dumar makes an appearance.

It's too late. Teachers are in the cafeteria running toward the fight. Someone blows a whistle. I get elbowed and slip between two bodies struggling to stay upright. Falling to the floor would surely lead to being trampled.

As I move through the crowd I hear something crackling above. When I'm back to being shoulder to shoulder with everyone I look up and see two of the fluorescent lights sparking. That's just what we need—an electrical fire on top of the gas fire we had last week.

I give up trying to reach Trigga because Mr. Strickman—the gym teacher/god from the Majestic—has just scooped him up by the collar, which is no easy task. I know that Trigga will be in good hands and get a fair shot at punishment since Strickman's there. Otherwise, Dumar with his biased opinions of class and status in this town would have Trigga and Fats expelled.

My bigger concern now is the sparking lights. I keep

staring at them, watching the sparks grow, spewing faster, dropping to the floor where hundreds of students still converge. Krystal comes up beside me. "We've got trouble," she says and is looking up just like me.

"Electrical issues?"

"No, supernatural issues," Krystal says, tugging on my shirt sleeve. "Take a look."

She's looking at those twins again and I'm about to tell her she's obsessed when I see one of them pucker her lips like she's about to give someone a kiss. I don't remember if this is Isis or Ivy, but whichever one it is, she's looking up at the lights just like me. Only she keeps her lips puckered and out comes this frosty mist that shoots right up to the ceiling, freezing the sparking light fixture.

"Crap," Krystal whispers. "Did you just see that?"

I nod, then realize Krystal's probably still staring at the ceiling like I am and figure speech will work better. "I think so."

When the fixture is completely frozen—I mean icicles are now hanging like eerie crystalline necklaces from the entire rectangular light—my gaze slides from the ceiling to the floor where I watch those look-a-likes walk toward us.

"You should talk to someone about the electricity in this school," the one with still-frosted blue lips says.

The other one is smiling, her eyes raking over Krystal like she's going to be her next meal. "We figured it was best if we help out around here."

"How?" I start to say then shake my head. "Where did you come from?"

"Tell her where we came from, Isis," the blue-lipped girl who I now assume is Ivy, says.

Isis takes a step toward Krystal, lifts a strand of her hair and runs it through her fingers. "I'd say we came from the same place as you, but that would be our lie. You see, we're stronger and better at this than you will ever be."

"Is that some type of challenge?" I ask because it certainly sounds like one and I'm really not in the mood to back down right now. The adrenaline flowing rampantly throughout the cafeteria is spurring me on. My heart's pumping wildly in my chest and everything inside me itches, anticipates.

Ivy laughs and Isis joins her. "You wouldn't stand a chance against us."

"Wanna try that theory out?" Krystal asks from beside me. Apparently the adrenaline rush must be in the air.

"Clear the cafeteria," someone yells on the loudspeaker. "All students should be en route to fifth period class. Any lurkers will be prosecuted."

Prosecuted? That had to be Dumar with his over-the-top seriousness.

From behind I feel a hand on my shoulder and feel a slap of relief when I look up to see Dylan.

"Is everything all right?" he asks, looking from Ivy to Isis.

Both girls take a simultaneous step back, their smiles never faltering. "Everything is just fine," they say in unison, making me want to cringe.

They walk away without further incident, then Dylan walks me to my next class. I don't get a chance to ask Krystal what she thinks of the eerie twins because Dylan sticks to me like glue. When he drops me off at class, he kisses me on the lips. I linger a little longer than need be hoping to feel something from him. Not necessarily read his mind but at least pick up on some emotion he's feeling.

Nothing.

I get a chill with that thought.

A chill like the one I got watching Ivy Langhorne spit frost to the ceiling.

Three days later there's a memorial service for Twan. It's at Krystal's church, which is small but a good portion of the town crowds into the tiny building.

We all sit together, me and Krystal on either side of Sasha and Jake next to Krystal. Jake's dad is here but he's standing in the back, letting Twan's family and friends take the bulk of the seats. On a table draped in a black cloth sits a brass urn, behind it a picture of Twan, smiling. Looking at it brings a pang to my chest. Twan smiled a lot.

Most times when I read his mind he was thinking of something happy, something about Sasha. I believe he loved her, really loved her and that makes my chest hurt more. Just about everyone is wearing black today, me included. There's this fog drifting in my mind, like a stormy day. It just hangs there, heavy and solid, blocking just about everything but grief.

The organist, a heavy-set black man with a receding hairline and seemingly magical fingers, plays some melancholy tune. Sasha's shoulders shake constantly, her tears flowing like a summer storm. Heads are bowed and the room's silent but for the organ and random sniffles.

In the first row Twan's grandmother cries, unable to be consoled. Two other ladies huddle around her, passing tissues and rubbing her back. My eyes water just watching the exchange. I want to scream, can feel it bubbling in the back of my throat. Of course it doesn't come out. Seems my emotions get stuck in times of distress, which is crazy since I'm a beacon for everybody else's emotions, storing them like a squirrel does nuts. I've tried and tried forever to understand my power and what I'm supposed to do with it. Today, of all days, I feel more useless than I ever have.

I know it shouldn't be about me. I should be remembering Twan and be here for my friend who's suffering a tremendous loss, but my mind's drifting. It's rolling over unanswered questions and suppositions. And I keep hearing that female voice, the one that calls my name like she's about to tell me something then vanishes completely. For once, I'd like it to finish the sentence, to say what it has to say because something tells me it's important.

The preacher climbs into the pulpit and opens a big black bible. He begins to read a scripture and I can hear Krystal reciting the words. She believes the words in that book, believes what the preacher is reading wholeheartedly. That belief has given her some kind of peace. Just like Jake's confrontation and decision has given him a calming spirit, as well. I wonder if there's peace somewhere for me, some semblance of normal that I can grasp that'll make all this seem worth it.

A mumbled "Amen" by everyone in the room signals the end of the service and people line up to see Twan's grandmother. Sasha opts not to go, which I think might be best. She's seen his grandmother a couple of times since the accident and talked to her alone. A public visit might break both of them.

I lead the line of Mystyx filing out of the church into the cloudy afternoon. The air is thick with humidity and my dress immediately sticks to my back. I think we're riding with Jake—me and Krystal, that is. There's something called a repass at Twan's grandmother's house but I don't know if we're attending. Sasha mentioned she'd just like to go home and lie down. Mouse drove her to the church so I assume he's waiting near her car to take her back. Maybe I'll go back home, too, do some reading on empathic abilities or something like that.

The three uniformed police officers standing at the corner look like they have another idea entirely.

"Jake Kramer?" One of the officers calls to Jake.

There's a tense moment when all four of us just stand still, looking. Then Jake steps away from us and toward the cops.

"Yes?" he answers.

"We'd like to ask you a few questions," the officer says.

Krystal immediately breaks away from the group, leaving me to hold Sasha steady and keep an eye on the cops and Jake.

"What about?" Jake asks, peeling off the suit jacket he wore.

"About Antoine Watson. We understand you were the last person to see him alive."

"We all were," I say, hoping this helps to not single Jake out in this mess.

One officer cuts his eye at me. It's not a friendly look.

"We'd like to talk to you alone, Jake," the first officer insists.

"You're not talking to him alone," Harry Kramer says, touching my shoulder as he moves past me and Sasha to get to Jake. When he stands by his son he touches a hand to his shoulder and looks directly at the officers. "We'll both come to the station."

Mr. Kramer always talks in that no-nonsense way. He's a big man with a dominating aura that greets you about five minutes before you actually see him coming. Even though Mr. Kramer isn't supernatural, I'm betting Jake gets his quiet strength from his dad.

"We just have a few questions," the officer says.

Mr. Kramer nods. "Then this won't take long."

Jake digs into his pocket and pulls out his keys. He tosses them to Krystal and says, "Use my truck to take Lindsey home. I'll come by your house later to pick it up."

Krystal catches the keys and nods. She's still a little out of breath after running to get Mr. Kramer.

We watch them disappear down the sidewalk, the police getting into their cruisers and Mr. Kramer and Jake climbing into Mr. Kramer's truck.

"They think he had something to do with it," Krystal says quietly.

"We all did," I admit sadly.

"It's my fault," Sasha says, wiping her latest batch of tears from her eyes. "I should have stayed away from him. I should have known I could never have a normal relationship when there's nothing normal about me."

"That's not true," I say quickly. "We all have some normal in us." At least I'm desperately hoping we do. "We just have this task we have to fulfill then we can get on with our lives."

"But in the meantime it gets to kill anyone we love?"

Sasha asks. Her eyes search mine for a real truthful answer that I don't have.

"Not if we step up our game," Krystal says. "There are others like us. I know he's sent them. It's time we get more proactive."

She's talking about those twins, the ones that eye me every time they see me. They're powerful, I can tell because I saw it with my own eyes and because I feel it when they're near. I can't read their minds but I feel their evil, feel it brewing inside them, bubbling just beneath the surface. Krystal's right, it's time to step up our game.

"I don't want to do this," Sasha says. "I just don't want to do this anymore."

She runs across the street into the parking lot where Mouse stands with her car.

"She's just upset right now," Krystal says. "She'll be all right."

"I hope so," I mumble, watching Sasha go, feeling like the wave of sadness has only just begun for us.

seventeen

Divided

"I like looking at you," Dylan says, his breath a warm whisper over my face.

We're lying in the grass at the far end of the football field. We'd both practiced hard and long today and when it was over, had collapsed here instead of heading directly to his car. The sun's wavering, falling deeper into the sky. It's warm and there's a heavy breeze that blows every ten minutes or so.

Dylan is holding my hand, his head turned so that he's looking right at me—because my head is turned, too. It's been a tough time in the two weeks since Twan's death. Sasha's more distant than she was when it first happened. Jake's been trying to get us together to talk about our next move but she keeps brushing us off. Krystal's really worried about her. Jake's getting angry and me, I don't know. A part of me wants to deal with Charon and this evil he's trying to bring forth, but another part just wants to live. I think that's because I don't feel like I've really lived since my parents' deaths. Most times I feel like I'm still stuck in life a year ago.

Except when I'm with Dylan.

He makes me feel different, happier, I think.

"I like looking at you, too." And I do, except there's this nagging thought in the back of my mind each time I do. His eyes are beautiful, too beautiful.

"I want you to be my girl," he says.

I'm not real surprised since in my mind I was thinking we were already a couple. It's cute that he's making it official though.

"I can do that," I respond because I don't really know what else to say. Dylan's my first official boyfriend. He was my first kiss and as he moves closer and butterflies dance around in my stomach, I have this fleeting thought that he may be my first in something else.

This feels like the most natural thing in the world when Dylan rolls over on top of me. So when my arms lift and twine around his neck, my body scooting so that it fits perfectly with his, I'm not surprised by the little moan of pleasure that slips from my throat. I'm sure every exciting emotion I'm feeling right now is my very own, the tickling sensation in the pit of my stomach, the slow, steady heat building and stretching throughout my body—it's all mine.

Out of the blue I remember something I've read: kissing passionately for ninety seconds causes the pulse rate to race. It also increases the level of hormones in the blood, thus reducing life by one minute. If that's really the case then I'm certainly ready to die young.

His lips touch mine in a gentle swoosh. I lift my head, greedy for more. He smiles as if he knew I'd do just that. I smile back because his smile's so enticing. Then I kiss him. I touch my lips to his once, then twice, then hard the third time, hungrily. He kisses me back taking the action deeper than I first anticipated. I gasp, parting my lips as my heart hammers in my chest, intense heat threatening to consume me now.

Dylan's hands are on my shoulders, moving down my body. I'm squirming beneath him trying to find a spot that eases this building need. Nothing works.

That ten-minute breeze blows and fills me with the scent of outside, the tinge of the sun and its dying rays, the blades of fresh-cut grass and musty teenagers. I'm in a zone, I guess you could call it, wrapped in Dylan's arms, loving the feel of him on me, his lips on mine. Then I hear it, a loud rumble. The ground shakes but Dylan keeps kissing me. The rumbling grows louder and it feels like the Earth is trembling beneath us.

Dylan doesn't make a move to get off me but I turn my head to the side, moving my lips from his. I'm looking around and see the perfect sunny sky has turned a dark dull gray. The stifling air that had just blown is now a frigid, wet breeze.

I push against his shoulders and Dylan reluctantly pulls back. He's looking down at me and his once-perfect eyes now appear as stormy as the sky.

"What's the matter with you?" I ask, lifting a hand to his face.

"I—" He stops, clenches his lips tightly together. "I can't stop—"

"Well, what do we have here?" a female voice speaks.

I jump like I've just been caught shoplifting. It's an effort because Dylan moves at a much slower pace like he doesn't even care that someone's looking at us practically having sex on the football field.

Struggling to stand up and brush grass off my clothes at the same time, I'm almost knocked over by the intense wave of hatred that slams into me. Gulping for air I finally right myself and look at the twins. My palms start to sweat because I know this is going to be bad.

"Dylan, you bad boy," says the one I'm pretty sure is Isis now because her eyes are that funny-colored brown, almost like a cat or an animal. Right now they look like they're filled with something else, like flecks of orange and gold.

"We were just foolin' around," he says and his voice is different, a little lower.

I look at him but I can't see his face because he's moved in front of me. I want to push past him to confront the girls myself so he won't find out they have some kind of power but when I put my hand on his shoulder he uses an arm to push me back.

"Foolin' around with the help," Isis says, then makes a tsking sound. She's wearing jean shorts and a red top that wraps around her body and I guess ties in the back.

Ivy has on a similar outfit but it's a baby-blue top and white bottoms for her. It's weird how they move in perfect sync. When Ivy crosses her arms over her chest Isis does the same, at the same exact time. Isis stands with her right foot forward, her left hip poked out. Ivy has an identical stance.

"It's cool. You two can go on home now," Dylan says and I get the feeling he knows them personally.

That doesn't mean he knows about their powers. I wish I didn't know, but I guess it makes sense to be forewarned.

"Go home? Oh, no, it looks like things are just getting heated up here."

Isis says this and I have to blink twice before I accept what I'm seeing. Those flecks in her eyes are beginning to look like flames.

"Who are you two?" I can't help but ask. Stepping to the side I try to get a better look at both of them. Not like they're going to have *supernatural* tattooed on their foreheads or anything, but I'm just looking for something, anything, that can tell me exactly what I'm dealing with.

I'm looking for an *M* birthmark like the one I have, the one the other Mystyx have. Of all their skin that's bared I don't see any mark. And if I remember correctly, I didn't see one that day at the pool when they wore even less.

"Me?" Isis asks in a fake, candy-sweet voice. "You want to know who I am?"

My insides churn and I'm engulfed by dread. Something's not right. This whole situation isn't right. Warning bells are playing a symphony in my head, sending messages to my feet to get the hell out of here. But my feet obviously missed the memo. I don't even know I'm nodding my head in answer to her question.

Ivy smiles, slow and wide, her eyes sparkle like snow-flakes and I can't look away from her. Without another word of warning Isis lifts a hand, pointing a finger at the scoreboard. From that finger a line of fire bursts free, aiming and landing accurately over the word *HOME*.

"Stop it!" Dylan yells, stepping toward Ivy.

"Dylan! No!" I scream, visions of Twan being thrown by that creature pressing into my brain. "Stay away from her!"

I should be running, but moving is not in the cards as I stand there staring and yelling instead. Isis moves to stand right beside me.

"Such a naive little thing you are," she quips.

Her words don't concern me. I'm Asian-American, I've been called much worse. But when she steps behind me and I feel a blast of cold air over my right shoulder, everything inside me stills. A slow-building wave of frost almost precisely traces the path Isis just drew of fire, splashing into the HOME block and freezing the entire scoreboard.

Dylan pulls me by the arm moving me away from Ivy. "I said that's enough. Go home!" he yells at them and I'm positive he knows them now. They're looking at each other with that kind of familiarity that would normally make a girlfriend jealous—especially a new girlfriend that's having her first experience with a boy. But what I'm feeling looking at them together is much uglier than jealousy.

Isis turns and her eyes are totally orange now, like they're circles burning in her head. I cringe but Dylan stands firm, his body almost blocking me completely.

"I'm doing what has to be done," she says to him.

"You're going overboard," he retorts. "I've got this under control."

Ivy saunters over to stand beside Isis. Her lips are discolored, like a dusky gray, I figure it's from blowing all that cold air. "You've got something under control," she says. "I'm just not so sure it's the right thing."

Dylan turns to me and says, "Go to my car, Lindsey. I'll be there in a minute."

"No. I'm staying," I say adamantly. Like hell I'm going to

leave him with the psycho twins. Besides, he doesn't seem at all surprised by what they can do.

"Let her stay and play with us, Dylan," Ivy says in a sugary-sweet voice that makes me want to punch her.

"Why don't you two leave?" I suggest and feel the pounding of my heart magnified in my chest.

I don't know what's in their minds at all, their eyes are too freakish for me to glare into to try to get a thought. And absolutely nothing is emanating from them besides evil. Pure, unadulterated evil that's shocking to me because they're so young, too young to be this bad already.

"You're a bold one, aren't you?" Isis asks, attempting to walk around Dylan toward me.

Dylan moves with her so that he's still in front of me. But I'm tired of him trying to protect me. So I move quickly in the opposite direction coming face-to-face with Ivy.

"Do you have a problem with me?" I ask because I learned a long time ago—and again just a few months ago with Jake—to face bullies head-on.

Now Isis and Ivy just moved to Lincoln and until today, hadn't really posed any type of threat to me. But I get the feeling they don't like me, whether it's because I'm a Mystyx or just a girl that Dylan's interested in, I have no idea. Whatever the reason I plan to get to the bottom of this right now.

Ivy chuckles. "I have such a big problem with you."

In a flash she lunges for me but I'm quicker. Ducking and rolling over the grass I escape her approach. But she's coming at me again so I jump to my feet then do a series of cartwheels that takes me farther away from her. She's coming after me and now so is Isis.

Right now I wish my power was more active instead of mental. Their minds are blocked by something so I can't even get a read on them so I can counteract whatever they try to do to me. All I can do is ward them off physically, which doesn't look like it's going to work very well with two against one.

But just as quickly as I see them running toward me I watch as both of them are lifted from the ground and thrown a few feet in the opposite direction of where I stand. Like a blur of wind I'm thrown back a couple steps when Jake steps in front of me. I don't know where he came from but I'm glad he's here.

"Stay behind me," he says and I listen because over his shoulder I see Dylan heading toward us and he doesn't look happy at all.

"I can protect her, Kramer," Dylan says when he's closer. The sky that was just graying is now totally dark. The air's sort of misty, not humid like it was before. There's a wind blowing, brushing over the grass, sending debris flying around the field.

"She doesn't need your kind of protection," Jake retorts.

Dylan shakes his head. He's closer now so I can see his eyes. They aren't the sparkling blue I'm used to seeing, but a duller shade, holding secrets that I've suspected for a while and so much more.

"You have no idea what you're walking into," Dylan says, his voice lifting over the sound of the wind.

"Go back to where you came from," Jake yells. "All of you!"

Isis and Ivy have flanked both sides of Dylan. They look

like a deadly threesome heading directly for us. Jake's ready to pounce; my arms ache at the feel of his strength building.

Touching the arm that doesn't have his birthmark I whisper, "Let's just go, Jake. We're not prepared for this."

Jake shakes his head vehemently. "I'm done running, Lindsey. We're all done running!"

He's right. Hadn't I just come to that conclusion with the twins? The difference now is that Dylan is involved.

"Then die as you should!" Isis shouts, sending a line of fire directly at us with her evil glare.

Jake stares the fire down, turning his head to the left when it's just a few inches from his face, sending the flames in an adjusted path to the left, as well. When he turns back to them Jake lifts his hands and pushes. All three of them fly backward, falling onto their backs. But that's only momentary—they're up faster than anything I've ever seen. Certainly faster than any human would have been able to achieve.

Isis looks down to the ground, freezing the once-thriving grass until my feet are slipping on the sheet of ice beneath them. Jake lifts a foot and stomps, the ice cracks, shatters and breaks beneath us. Then when I would have thought things couldn't get any worse, Dylan lifts his arm, points toward the scoreboard and sends a lightning bolt sizzling through the air. The scoreboard ignites in a bright display that almost resembles the Fourth of July fireworks then topples over, slamming to the ground in a sickening crash.

For a few seconds everything and everyone is absolutely still.

Then Dylan, holding his arms out to stop Ivy and Isis from doing anything else, says in a voice so dour and so deep I think there must be someone else inside him speaking, "You don't want this, Kramer. None of you are ready for this."

Dylan turns and pulls Isis and Ivy along with him. They walk away just like that. And while I hadn't felt anything from the three of them during this entire exchange except evil, now I'm feeling something else.

Grief. Because the person I thought Dylan was apparently does not exist.

That hideous emotion is back once again.

"He's one of them!" Jake yells, pounding the palm of his hand on the steering wheel.

We're in his truck and he's driving me home. He said he had to stay after to make up some work he'd missed while he'd been suspended, that's why he'd been walking across the field when he saw me.

"I think there's another explanation," I say, trying for a calm voice even though I'm shaking all over.

Jake's anger is vibrating throughout the cab of the truck, slamming into my temples like a sledgehammer. I'm nauseous and want to roll down the window, stick my head out and get some air.

"That's because you've got the hots for him. Let me tell you something, Lindsey, you need to stay away from him! From all of them until we figure out how to deal with them."

"We're never going to figure out how to do anything if we don't start asking questions."

"Who do you suppose we ask? The one who spits fire or the one who freezes everything she blows a kiss to?" The truck jerks us when Jake makes a turn. "Or how about we ask the guy you were just about screwing on the football field, who incidentally shoots lightning bolts from his fingertips?"

Everything he said sounds logical, in the midst of all the illogical things we deal with. I don't deny that it appears Dylan's one of them. But I want to know who "them" is.

"I just think that maybe they have some answers. You know we could use some of those."

"No, what we could use are some weapons or some really strong magicals on our side," he says. "We need all of us to be on board with getting rid of Charon once and for all."

"You're talking about Sasha now." I sigh because we've all been wondering what her state of mind truly is after Twan's death. "It's got to be hard dealing with all she's dealing with, Jake. Maybe we should just give her a little space."

He sighs and I know it's because he's thinking I'm right. Jake's known Sasha the longest, so he knows her struggles with her family. We all know what her father put her through, lying to her about her powers, selling our secret to Walter Bryant then leaving town without any notice or any calls since. Her mother's a basket case—for lack of a better term. The only one she has in the house is Mouse and he's stranger than we are.

"We're all dealing with a lot. We're teenagers, remember?"

I hate when Jake gets like this. When he can't see past his anger to be realistic. Or reality is what's making him so angry in the first place. His knuckles are white on the steering wheel and I reach out to touch a hand to his arm.

It's the arm with his birthmark and it's still warm. I should have figured that since my mark has been burning since the moment Ivy and Isis appeared on the field.

"We're not normal teenagers, Jake. That's what we really need to remember."

"Look, you just need to stay away from him and those girls."

"Weren't you the one to tell me back there that you weren't running anymore?" He doesn't answer. "Well, neither am I."

Jake pulls up in front of my house and slams his hands down on the seat. "I'm trying to protect you."

I put my hand on top of his. "We're going to protect each other. Don't worry," I say, then get out of the truck. I don't know why I'm so calm, why I'm not feeling as anxious and upset as Jake considering what I just found out.

But really, I think the moment I go into the house and shut the door behind me, it will hit me that I kind of knew that Dylan wasn't like other boys. I saw him first in my dreams, then he appeared on the bus. Thinking about it now, I saw the twins, too, in the dream about the train and my parents' deaths. If they're in that dream, they're connected somehow. I've known this, I guess, in the back of my mind. But it was so nice thinking there was more there between us, that maybe, just maybe this boy liked me for me.

After I shower I skip dinner. Salisbury steak and mashed potatoes aren't really appealing to me now. My calm has turned into melancholy that's weighing heavily on my shoulders. I don't want to cry. Still, I'm not thrilled with the fact that Dylan lied to me. I guess it can't be considered lying if he just neglected to tell me that his fingertips were electrical.

I'm guilty, too, if that's the case. I never told him that I can read minds and feel emotions.

It's late now, I've been lying in the bed for a while, just staring at the ceiling. It's not as cool as staring at the ceiling at Sasha's because mine doesn't have stars. But I'm not thinking about stars, anyway.

My cell phone vibrates and I reach for it.

out front. can u come down?

It's Dylan.

I shouldn't go. I know I shouldn't.

There's something going on with him and with those twins. They're not what I thought they were. I don't know what they are. I should be careful and yet all I can think about is seeing him again.

b right there

Before I can talk myself out of it I'm jumping off the bed and slipping my feet into my furry black slippers. I have on pajama pants and a tank so I feel like I'm decent enough. As I walk down the stairs I think of what Sasha would say.

"Are you crazy? You're going to meet him after what he just did?"

I let out a nervous chuckle because her voice sounds so serious and so Sasha even in my head. I know it's crazy. I know I shouldn't be doing it. But I can't help it. It's like that cupcake your mother tells you not to take after she's just baked and iced them. No matter what you do you keep ending up in the dining room staring at the tray of cupcakes wondering how good they'll taste. Until finally, you pick one up and take a bite.

It's either gloriously good and you rub your stomach as the sweet perfection goes down—or your mother comes up behind you as soon as you take that bite and you're totally busted.

I don't know how it'll end as I sneak out of the house once more and head down the hill to where I see Dylan's car waiting in the dark. All I know is that right now going to him is too good to resist.

eighteen

Unwelcomed Guests

HE'S leaning against the car, his jeans crisp, T-shirt molded to his chest. His hands rest on the hood as he watches me walk toward him.

I take my time with these last few steps, still second-guessing myself but knowing it's something I have to do.

"Why didn't you tell me?" is the first thing out of my mouth.

"Why didn't you tell me?" is his reply.

I sigh. "So what now? We're two supernatural freaks dating?"

He shrugs. "I don't know how to explain it."

That's funny, I don't, either. There may not even be an explanation, but what does that mean for us? I can't figure out how to say this to him without sounding desperate or crazy.

"I wouldn't have let them hurt you," he says then. "I'd never let anyone hurt you."

I'm looking at him now, really staring at everything about him. From his unruly hair down to his broad shoulders and arms roped with veins. His tapered waist and long legs, then I go back to his hands and my gaze rests there for a minute.

"Why me?" I ask and don't really know if I'm asking why he chose me or why I have these powers. Maybe the answer is one and the same.

He shrugs. "I don't know. It just is."

"That may not be a good thing," I reply.

"And it may be the best thing."

He leans forward, reaches out an arm and wraps it around my waist. When he pulls me to him I gasp. Our bodies are pressed solidly together. And his lips find mine.

It's like they're meant to touch, to twine and to mingle. There's no indecision here, no second-guessing myself or wondering what the others will think. All I know right now is bliss. I'm kissing Dylan. He's kissing me.

And no supernatural power could be as strong as we are together, at this moment.

"My dad came home last night," Sasha says before sticking a carrot into her mouth and munching down on it.

None of us know what to say so we don't say anything. We're in the cafeteria, watching the daily humdrum of activity. There's less students here because we have about a week and a half left in school. They really should have just let us out early since the C hallway is still blocked off after the fire.

I don't see the twins or Dylan anywhere but I'm trying not to let that worry me. Jake hasn't said anything about what happened yesterday but from the way he keeps looking at me, I know it's just a matter of time. Sasha's little announcement is definitely taking precedence.

"He talked to my mom about moving. She wants me to stay and finish up my senior year," she continues.

Krystal nods like she understands but she's really thinking of what else Mr. Carrington may have said upon his return. "That makes sense," she says.

"Sure. It's not fun transferring schools and in your senior year it's probably worse," I add from my own experience.

"Did he say anything about Walter Bryant? About Project S?"

Jake's the bold one today, and most days, for that matter. He asks the question we're all thinking.

Sasha shakes her head. "He said he was away on business. But I went through his suit jacket pocket when he and my mom went out to dinner. The plane ticket stub said Barrow, Alaska."

"We thought that was where they went," Jake says, nodding. "It's dark there for a couple weeks out of the year. It's a great hiding place for exiled demons."

"But that's in like November or something," Krystal says.

I nod. "It's during the Autumn Equinox. Because of where they're positioned on Earth they get less sunlight during that time. I don't understand how that would help them though."

"I think they're trying to create their own supernaturals," Sasha says.

Krystal almost chokes on her soda. "What?"

"Like clones?" I ask.

Sasha nods affirmatively.

"That's just great." Jake sighs. "Like we don't have enough to deal with."

"I saw some email messages on his computer, too. Some

of them were with Mr. Bryant. I think they're trying to get funding for the project. One scientist guy sounds really skeptical though."

"Well, that's one good thing," Krystal says, putting her trash into a brown paper bag. She's frowning when she looks up. "What if they do get funding? There's got to be some idiot out there on the same page as Bryant."

"You think so?" Sasha asks.

"Sure. Didn't the government create the Majestic 12 to investigate alien invasions? They knew then that there were people on Earth that weren't normal humans. All the efforts they've made over the years were just to cover it up. There are definitely more people out there interested in supernatural activity."

"She's right. There are people who are still studying this phenomenon. All they'd have to do is find the right person with the right size bank account," I reply dismally.

"This is not good," Jake says.

"Tell me about it," Sasha adds. "I do not want to be in the same house with him. He's a hypocrite and my mother can't see that. Plus he keeps watching me like he expects me to bring the entire house crashing down around us with my power. I'll be so glad when I graduate so I can get out of there."

Sasha's father is not pleased nor accepting of her power. I remember her telling us how she threatened her father with unveiling her power to the world so he would let Jake and his family stay in their house. Come to think of it, that makes Mr. Carrington's return to Lincoln even more dangerous. And not just for the Mystyx as a unit, but for Sasha.

Feeling bad for her I figure switching subjects might be good. "You decide where you're going to school?" I ask.

She shakes her head. "No. But it doesn't matter. I just want to get as far away from Lincoln and my parents as I can. I'll go to Timbuktu if I have to."

She means it. Sasha's really fed up. Tension pours from every word and action. I don't even have to look at her to know she's about to explode.

"We have more bad news," Jake says, and he looks directly at me.

I clear my throat because it's my responsibility to tell them. I just hope they understand.

"Yesterday those twins approached me. Both of them have power. One spits frost and the other fire," I say quickly.

Krystal sits back in her chair and sighs. "Are you serious?"

Sasha tucks her hair back behind her ears. "And?"

It's a solitary word, spoken in a slow and precise way. She acts like she knows, but I know she doesn't. She's suspected all along and I really hate to admit that she was right. Partially, at least.

"Dylan has power, too," I say softly.

"He shoots lightning bolts from his fingers," Jake adds. "The girls tried to attack Lindsey. When I showed up they were demonstrating their talents on the scoreboard out back."

"Dylan?" Krystal says, her voice almost a whisper.

She's thinking how sorry she is for me, how awful this must make me feel. But it doesn't. I mean, I guess it should, but I feel like there's another explanation.

"He's not evil," I say quickly.

Sasha slams a hand on the table. "Really, Lindsey? How can you sit there and say that? Jake just said they attacked you."

I'm shaking my head because she's got it all wrong. "The twins tried to attack me. Jake fought them off. Dylan tried to protect me."

She's not buying it. Sasha's eyes narrow on me. "Before or after he shot lightning bolts from his fingers?"

"He's not evil. I would know. I would feel it," I insist. And I believe what I'm saying with my whole heart. I don't feel evil from Dylan. I don't feel anything outside of the pleasure, but I'm not about to tell them this.

"Are you crazy?" Sasha asks, trying not to raise her voice but even more agitated now than she was before.

Krystal clears her throat. "I think she's in love."

Sasha throws up her hands. "That's just great."

"I think they're here to distract us. I think they're working with Charon," Jake says.

"Why? They could be Mystyx like us," I offer, trying to ignore the heated vibes coming from Sasha. I know that a lot of it is because she lost Twan and she was in love with him. I don't want to hurt her anymore with my situation with Dylan, but I don't want to judge him too harshly, too quickly, either.

"Does Dylan have the mark?" Krystal asks.

I shrug. "I don't know." Sasha looks at me skeptically.

"I haven't seen a mark on him. And I didn't see any on the twins at the pool, either." Most of their bodies were exposed that day and I remember staring at them for a while when they were at the bar. No mark.

"Maybe she's the one starting the fires," Krystal says.

We're all quiet for a moment because I don't think any of us were connecting the twins to the two fires that had taken place.

"Then which one of them killed Twan?" Sasha asks. "Which one of them summoned that beast that killed him? I want to know right now!"

Everything inside me hurts, from my head to my feet. I can't distinguish one pain from the other and breathing has now become a chore. It's Sasha's pain, her grief that's ripping through me yet again.

"I think the beast is here for me," I tell her, knowing she's not going to like any answer I give.

"Then why didn't it take you!" she yells and stands up.

"Sasha," Krystal whispers.

Her lips clench together tightly and she sits back down, placing her palms flat on the table. "I can't do this anymore," she whispers. "I just can't."

And neither can I.

My entire body is shaking with Sasha's emotions. Jake's furious and ready to act. Krystal is confused. I'm afraid.

This is all too much and I'm the one who gets up this time, leaving the rest of them at the table to look after me as I run through the cafeteria.

nineteen

Help

I'M a coward.

I wish I wasn't but I am. I've stayed in my room for four whole days, not going to school, not even looking out the window. Whatever is out there I don't want to see or feel. Mostly feel.

I have only one body, one mind, one heart and yet it feels for so many. I'm five foot two and weigh ninety-two pounds soaking wet and full from Thanksgiving dinner. I have allergies that peak when summer turns to fall and I just graduated into a modest B cup. I'm not cut out to hold the emotions of an entire school.

Four days ago I thought I would choke and die from Sasha's anger and grief alone. That didn't even include the table across from us where Olivia and the rest of the cheerleaders sat, their feelings of superiority and unbridled perkiness gnawing at the back of my brain. Across the cafeteria were the goths, their minds full of depressing thoughts that had me craving Paxil. And somewhere in the midst of all this, my heart's breaking—no, it's filling to completeness with the glow of my first love. Then it's aching with the possibility that my first love might be demonic.

When I came home I ran straight upstairs, Beesley right behind me. As I plopped back onto the bed the stupid dog began licking my fingers. I wanted to pull away and yell for the mangy beast to get out of my room, but once again I couldn't speak.

So I started thinking, when does my voice disappear? When am I—the usually talkative one of the group—rendered completely speechless? It's emotional, like everything about these powers seems to be, it's linked to our emotions. My emotions. Not the ones I inherit from anyone else, the ones that are all mine. Namely the fear and the grief.

I'm still grieving for my parents and I'm afraid of what that means.

It's taken me four days to figure that out. One hour and one hundred and seventy-five dollars a session with a shrink probably would have solicited the same results. But my way is much more rewarding.

Today I've at least showered and now sit on my bed wondering what the revelation will mean to the big picture of my life. I haven't talked to anyone in these days, only Mrs. Hampton, who, as it turns out, is very knowledgeable and not necessarily bad to talk to.

I've decided I can't hide forever, no matter how appealing the thought is. Actually, after I've had this solitude and sort of purged myself of everyone else's thoughts and feelings, I kind of feel a lot better.

Beesley's lying on the floor by my door where he's seemed to park himself these past four days. He's Mrs. Hampton's dog but for some reason has taken a liking to me all of a sudden. I stopped arguing with the dirty mutt days ago, figuring it was a waste of my newfound energy.

I'm going out today. Actually, it's night since I've sat here thinking about my next move for so long. I have on black leggings, a white T-shirt and white sneakers.

Balance, that's what I'm aiming for.

My first steps lead me to the window where I twist the rod that opens my blinds. I've been in the dark, too, did I mention that? Well, at least I waited until nighttime to make my debut. My eyes still blink, and cringe slightly at the adjustment. My street is quiet, desolate, as usual. Nobody comes near this house because it's haunted. My lips spread into a smile as I start to believe the stories myself. This house is haunted by a Guardian, an empath and a mangy old mutt that can't even remember how to bark.

I flatten my palm against the window and close my eyes, preparing myself to leave this room, to step outside and brave whatever is out there waiting for me.

"Own your power."

I jolt at the sound of the voice then turn slowly. She's sitting in the center of my bed, her legs crossed. Her hair is pulled up in a high ponytail that makes her look younger, more innocent. And she smiles, something I've missed seeing.

"What are you doing here?" I ask, taking a step closer to the bed.

"Teaching you how to be a real Mystyx," Sasha says with that know-it-all tone of hers that's just a tad shy of being sarcastic.

The door to my room is closed. I don't see her car out front. She's either teleported or astral projected here. I keep staring to figure out which one.

"For the record," she says, "I'm at home, lying in my bed.

My television is on for good measure and turned up loud. Mom knows how much I like to watch reality television. Dad hates it. He won't come into my room for that reason and because he doesn't want me asking any questions."

"So you astral projected to my bedroom," I say, taking a step toward her. "For what?"

"I told you I'm here to help you stand up and be what you were meant to be."

"What makes you think I'm not already doing that?"

She chuckles, throwing her head back so her long, tanned neck is completely visible. Yeah, I'm jealous because she's not only pretty and stylish, but she tans better than a bottle on the shelf at the Walgreen's and all the tanning beds at Teri's Tanning Salon. I'd hate her if I didn't like her so much.

"Yeah, hiding out in this haunted old house with that funky dog is really living up to your supernatural expectations," she quips and I think I might not like her so much.

"I needed some time."

"I know how that is." She nods. "So you've had it, now let's get to work."

"You can't teach me how to use a power that's not yours."

"Very true," she says, uncrossing her legs and letting them dangle off the side of the bed.

She looks like she's really here but I know if I touch her I'm not going to feel body. This is a projection of Sasha. Sure it's talking, laughing, smiling, joking, just like Sasha. But it's not her real body. Still I must admit I'm glad to have her here in any form.

"But I can tell you how I managed to embrace my power." She touches her chest then slides her hand down to her midriff where her *M* is scrawled. "You see, Lindsey, this is a part of us. The goddess created us before we were even a part of creation. That's a really big deal. And as long as you go around acting like this is one of your useless facts or some birth defect like an unsightly mole or an eleventh toe, you're never going to get it."

I plop down on the bed beside her because after my four days of solitude I thought I had finally figured everything out. Apparently, in the World According To Sasha Carrington, I've missed it completely.

"I appreciate my power, if that's what you're saying."

She shakes her head, her hair swishing as she does. "I'm not saying you don't appreciate it, I'm saying you refuse to learn how to use it. There's a reason you have this power, a purpose for it in the grand scheme of things."

"I know that."

"So do you know how to use it?"

I'm about to answer her, to tell her that I think I need to get my emotions in check first. But that doesn't sound right now, after listening to her. She sounds like she has a totally different answer and I'm curious to hear it.

"I can read minds and feel emotions. How do I use that to fight a demon?" I ask out loud the question I've asked myself over and over again. Out loud it sounds different.

"He wants what we all have inside us. Our power, our youth holds him back. It proves perseverance and strength in the human race. It gives good the upper hand."

"And he doesn't want that."

"Nope. He wants us vulnerable, distracted." She gets quiet. "Hurting."

"I'm so sorry about Twan," I say, really wanting to reach out and touch her.

She nods again, this time so swiftly I know it's to keep from crying.

"I don't know why he had to die. Maybe because he was too close to us. Maybe somehow Charon knew Twan knew about him. I don't know the answer." She takes a deep breath then blows it out. "I just know that if I don't see this through then he died in vain. And I'm not about to let that happen."

"I think there's something else going on with me," I finally confide in someone.

"Like what? Is it the talking thing? Because yeah, you talk a lot. But we're getting used to it."

I can't help but grin. "No. It's something else." It's my turn to take a deep breath and close my eyes. Then I reopen them and say real fast, "When I stare into someone's eyes and read their thoughts I feel something else."

"Something like what?"

"Control."

"As in you can control what they're thinking?"

"I think so."

I hadn't really tried out my theory but at cheerleader practice one day I was looking at Davanna, staring into her big brown eyes. I was actually wondering how she managed to get such perfectly and naturally (I asked her) arched eyebrows and long curly lashes. I would personally kill for one or the other. I'm not greedy.

So anyway, Davanna had looked up, caught me staring and just smiled. I felt that smile like a ray of sunshine on the gloomiest day. It permeated every pore of my body.

She was thinking of being happy to be on the cheerleading squad, of having great friends and a perfect 4.0 GPA. She had everything going for her and she was looking forward to every moment of her life. I remember resenting her that feeling of contentment and wishing I could borrow just a little bit for myself. Again, greed is not one of my attributes.

And as I thought of what I wanted, Davanna's smile wavered. It was just a little bit, her bottom lip trembling ever so slowly it wavered. Now instead of bright happiness her eyes were a little clouded, a lot confused.

Realistically she could have been looking that way wondering why I was still staring at her. But something inside me said that wasn't it.

"What if I could influence someone's thoughts? If my insight into their mind could actually control what they were thinking, change it somehow?"

Sasha sits quietly.

Drumming my fingers on my thighs I think about what I just said and whether or not it makes sense. For days now I've been thinking it was crazy. Sasha's silence makes me believe she's thinking the same thing.

"If you can control his mind you could stop him from wanting evil to win," she says. "That would definitely make you a colossal threat to Charon's gameplan."

"Just like Jake being a Vortex and you being able to see the magical that nobody else can see and Krystal being able to bring the dead against him."

"Exactly."

I take another deep breath. "But it's not complete. There's something blocking me. Something—" My voice trails off.

"Something you need to resolve before it's time."

I nod. "You're right. I was just on my way to do that right now."

"To resolve whatever's blocking you?"

"No. Actually. I was going to go find Dylan."

"Oh, god, Lindsey! You cannot be serious! He's throwing freakin' electricity. Doesn't that scream demon to you?"

It should. I know it definitely should. I'm not naive, or at least I never believed myself to be. But when I look in Dylan's eyes that's just not what I see. It's not what I feel.

"There's something off about him and about those twins."

"Ah, yeah, they're possessed. Have you even turned on the television while you've been closed up in this house? In addition to all the tornadoes wreaking havoc in the Midwest—which, by the way, I think is releasing more of Charon's demonic spirits into this realm—Lincoln is under its own type of supernatural fire. And I use the term *fire* very literally. Maggie's was burned down, then right across the street that new nail salon that Kimmy Misner's mother just had to open to show off her new manicurist degree, was frozen. Yes, I said frozen to the point the windows exploded and the entire structure looks like something from that goofy *Ice Age* cartoon."

"Ivy and Isis," I whisper.

"Yes. It seems they're having the time of their lives in our town. The cops have questioned Jake after each incident."

"Why do they keep going to him?"

"Because he doesn't have the money to get a lawyer to sue their butts for harassment, that's why. Truth be told I think they're looking at all of us. They tried to talk to me but my mom said she'd get my dad's lawyers to call them.

They backed right off. And Krystal's mom is so embedded in the church I think they're afraid about being struck down by some higher being if they go near her."

"And they won't come here because they're afraid of the haunted house."

Sasha shrugs. "That and your vicious guard dog."

We both look toward the door where Beesley must realize we're talking about him and looks up, only one eye visible because his long, matted hair is stuck over the other one. We laugh.

"I'm going to see him anyway."

Sasha shakes her head.

"I don't think you should." Then she holds up a hand the second I'm about to say something else. "But I know you're just not going to listen to me. Why don't you take Cujo there with you?"

We look at Beesley again and crack up. "That's quite okay. I'll take my rocks instead."

Sasha nods. "Good idea. And call me the minute you get back."

"Agreed."

And just like that, Sasha's gone.

I feel much better after talking to her, much more focused on the part I play in this and even more eager to see Dylan. If I can read minds, can possibly control them, then his is the one I want to control first. He's not a demon and if he is, maybe I can change that.

Maybe.

twenty

Love Is Blind

can u meet me at the school?

MY fingers shake as I type the text. I'm nervous. Don't really know why. I know Dylan, so meeting up with him is cool. Sure, it's almost midnight but that's just a technicality. When the text is sent I lift my window and use the old drain pipe to guide me down the wall. I feel like Spiderman or Spidergirl. Wait, was there a Spidergirl?

I don't look down as I go—just keep my hands securely around the drain pipe, my feet scraping over the old bricks on my descent. It's times like these I wish me and Sasha could swipe powers. Teleporting would have been much easier than climbing down two stories.

When my feet finally touch the ground I give a grateful sigh. I hear heavy breathing in response and look up. Beesley's at the window, his big shaggy head hanging over the windowpane. "Go back to sleep," I whisper up at him. He looks at me like I'm speaking German or something. Dumb dog.

Walking down the hill away from the house I'm shrouded

by darkness. "He likes the dark," Mrs. Hampton's voice echoes in my head. I know what Charon likes but right now I don't care. This is not about him, it's about me and Dylan.

At the bottom of the hill my cell vibrates in my pocket and I grab it quickly.

sure. come alone.

Well, what did he think I was planning a midnight party or something? Of course, I'm coming alone. But just in case, I send a quick text to Sasha and Krystal.

meeting Dylan @ school

Never hurts to be cautious. I wish my caution would have led me to ask Sasha for a ride. As it is, I have to walk all the way to the school. In the dark. So not cool.

The streets are empty and everywhere I look I think I'm seeing something. A shadow. A blob of smoke. A raven. A creature. All things I've seen in the dark before. Again, not good.

Strangely I'm not afraid as I move through now-familiar streets. I know this town. I guess because now it's my home. I know the people and the trials it's been going through for months. I also know now that we can change all that. The revelation is invigorating and I walk a little faster.

Up ahead, in the distance, just as I can see the back field of the school, minus the scoreboard that I'm sure Davenport was amazed to find was gone, I hear laughter. Like he's welcoming me.

At my sides my fingers clench and unclench. There is a reason I'm doing this. A reason I'm confronting another supernatural in the middle of the night. It's a sad, sappy reason, but it's there nonetheless. What I feel for Dylan surpasses any amount of trepidation. I know there's something good in him. I have to believe that I could never fall for a guy who was total evil. I know that evil can be alluring, enticing, but not to me. It just couldn't be.

There's a side window to the school that's never locked, or so I heard. I wonder if that's where Dylan will meet me, if we'll go inside to talk or just stand out here. Something tells me that standing out here will only draw us a bigger audience. I'm walking across the field now. An eerie sort of power looms here. It's like a cloak hanging over the entire field and I shiver a little at its cold evilness. The laughter is on the wind, blowing over my school like pellets of ice. Crossing my arms over my chest I continue to walk purposefully. I don't see Dylan, don't feel his presence.

Just as that thought crosses my mind, a hand touches my shoulder and I jump so high I think I might now have flying powers.

"Jeez, you scared the crap out of me!" I yell, spinning around to look into Dylan's blue eyes.

"Sorry," he says, letting his hands fall to his sides.

The very first thing I notice, after my heart retreats from my throat and my hand settles over the racing beat against my chest, is that Dylan doesn't look right.

Sure, his eyes are still that fantastic blue that first attracted me to him, but that's all that's the same. His face is pale, like somebody got hold of a can of that weird dead people makeup and smeared it all over his face. I remember that makeup from my parents' funeral, remember the chalky effect it gave their once-happy faces. Dylan's looks worse because his thick, dark eyebrows and intense eye color stand out. His lips look chapped, like he's been in the North Pole walking at midnight without a coat instead of in Lincoln on a quiet spring night.

"What's the matter?" I ask, half wanting to take a step toward him, to touch his powdery-white skin. The other half asking if I'm out of my everlasting mind thinking of getting closer to something and apparently someone I know very little about.

He shakes his head. "Nothing. Where have you been?"

I shrug. "Home."

"I miss seeing you."

"You could have come by the house," I offer and watch carefully for his answer.

He looks away from me and I'm struck with yet another revelation.

"You can't come to my house, can you?" He doesn't answer. "That's why you always picked me up at the bottom of the hill. You can't get close to the house. Or is it that you can't get close because Mrs. Hampton is there and she's my Guardian?" The last comes out on a chilly whisper as Sasha's warnings couple with Mrs. Hampton's and for the first time I start to second-guess why I'm here.

"I can't warn you," he says, his gaze returning to mine. "I can't help you."

"Why? Who sent you? Who gave you power?" Because now I know without a doubt he's not a Mystyx. He's not like me.

His lips draw into a tight, painful-looking line. "I don't want to do this, Lindsey," he says and starts to look around.

The cool air picks up and I instinctively take a step back from him.

"I don't want to hurt you," Dylan says, taking each step with me. "I never wanted to hurt you."

"Then why?" I ask, my voice cracking because now, after all this time, fear is creeping up my spine like a deadly snake, inching toward my neck where I assume it'll grasp and finally kill.

The creature that came for me in the water wanted to kill me. Then the smoke creature at school charged for me. Twan's killer was actually aiming for me. And when the creatures didn't succeed, he sent Dylan. In the prettiest, deadliest package I'd ever seen.

My back slams against the brick wall of the school and I gasp. Dylan's right in front of me, his eyes the only part of him I recognize, the only part that still reaches out to me, to my heart.

"Dylan, don't," I whisper. "You can fight him. We can fight him."

His head is shaking but he's not speaking, he's just coming closer. Over his shoulder I glimpse a flash of light. It drops down from the dark sky in two shimmering bolts landing on either side of Dylan.

On the left it's a girl engulfed in flames, her hair blowing wild, head tossed back as she cackles. On the right, as if I even had to look, is another girl, hair flowing behind her, eyes, lips, cheeks and hands covered in a crystalline frost.

I'm reaching into my pocket, fiddling for my cell phone. If I can at least push the speed dial button somebody will know I'm in trouble. Sasha, Jake and Krystal are the only ones on my speed dial, the phone will dial one of them and they'll come. They'll come and help and maybe, just maybe, I won't die on this seemingly quiet spring night.

But just as I push the first button, Dylan's palm cups my cheek. It's an intense feeling, his cool skin against I guess my normal-temperature face. My entire body begins to chill, shiver and stiffen.

He leans closer like he's going to kiss me but his lips only brush mine then move in a torturously slow path toward my ear.

"I never meant to hurt you, Lindsey. Never."

I think I'm shivering but I can't tell. I can't move, am paralyzed from my neck down. There's absolutely no feeling and I have no idea how I'm still standing. All I know is that I can see him, I can feel inside—not a physical kind of feeling, but an emotional tug-of-war beginning.

Then Dylan picks me up, cradling me in his arms like I'm a baby. I can do nothing but stare up at him. I know that Isis and Ivy are there, that the wind must have picked up behind us because Dylan's soft curls blow at his ears. That flash of light appears again and I realize it's a lightning bolt and that it came from Dylan. He takes a step and suddenly it appears we're inside the bolt. There's a crackle of thunder and then we're gone. All I see is light, blinding light that finally makes my eyes close.

I don't know where I'm going or what will happen to me. And the last words I hear are from Dylan, in that eerily deep and perfect voice I'd come to love.

"I love you, Lindsey."

If I weren't paralyzed I might have swooned. If my heart weren't currently stuck in a headlock between my common sense and my desperate need for love and acceptance, I would be the happiest girl alive.

Instead, I'm here, in this place that I never wanted to be and the boy I've fallen in love with has just proven me wrong. Love must surely be blind.

twenty-one

Full Circle

"When we arrive and get unpacked we can go for dinner," Dad says, not even bothering to look up from his laptop.

Mom turns the next page in her book and smiles. "We'll order room service because you'll be too tired to go out."

"I want steak and baked potato," I chime in my dinner selection because they haven't bothered to ask me if I want to stay in the hotel or go out.

"They have a lovely filet there. The chef is from Monte Carlo, I think. He's fantastic," Mom says, still reading her book.

I'm tapping on the table, trying everything in my power to keep my eyes off the window with all the trees and scenery whizzing by. I don't know why Dad likes traveling by train. It makes me sick. I wish I had my iPod but I packed it in my suitcase by mistake. Huge mistake!

So I'm just sitting here looking at the people in the seats across the aisle from us. A woman and her two daughters. They're pretty, all of them. Just down the aisle is a man in a suit with his laptop on the table just like Dad's. I wonder if he works in politics or in some big office building that almost touches the sky. I wonder...

It tickles along my spine, like thousands of ants marching toward a corn chip or something edible. Squirming doesn't make it go away, it intensifies it. My ears feel like something's ringing inside my head. I want to grab my ears and cover them but I don't. Something keeps me still.

Then it happens.

The loudest, ghastliest sound I've ever heard vibrates through the car of the train. Fear paralyzes me. Mom and Dad look at me like they, too, hear this noise, like they know what I know.

"Lindsey," Mom says my name. "Honey, I want you to know something."

I shake my head because I can't answer her. I can't speak. If I do it'll hear me. Whatever made that sound will hear me and it'll know where I am. It's coming for me, I know it.

There's another roar and then the entire car jerks and rattles. Everybody is shifting and there are some screams. Mom reaches for my hand. "Lindsey, repeat after me, honey."

I see her lips moving but I can't hear what she's saying. The train is crashing, it's tumbling and we're sliding about the seats, falling and falling.

"Repeat after me," Mom says again then my hand slips from hers and my falling continues.

I slip through the doors going from one car to the other. A glance out the window shows the car is now upside down. The daylight I was just trying to avoid looking through the window is now dark. There's something out there, someone or something. My head and hips bang against seats, dislodged luggage and whatever else is floating through the train, then I slam into a door that leads out, my face flat against the glass.

On the other side another face slams into the glass. It's him, the boy with the dark hair and perfect blue eyes. He's looking right at me, smiling. Then he's not. His face peels away leaving hollow black holes until all that's left is a skeletal formation and those blue eyes.

My mouth opens, there is no scream there. But in my chest my heart beats a rapid beat threatening to break right through my rib cage. I push back from that window, closing my eyes. When I open them again the boy or the skeleton is gone. And through the window I see something else. It's big and ugly and stands on clawed feet. Its arms spring from a dinosaur-like upper body that leads to a head bigger than the White House, at least. As if it knows I'm looking at it, gawking at it, is more like it, it turns and stares at me.

It's come for me. It sees me.

I back up as far as I can go, as far as I can get from the creature. But it begins to run, charging right for the door.

And I hear Mom's voice in my head as if she's standing right next to me.

"Dark as night, large is fright. Take away this beast tonight. Repeat it, Lindsey." She says it again and again until I feel my lips moving in the same rhythm.

I don't actually hear the sound coming out of my mouth because I'm falling again, moving through the cars with pain racking my body. But my lips keep moving, they keep moving as if they're reciting the same words Mom said in my head.

My eyes shoot open, almost painfully so. I know I'm

awake and the dream is over when air whooshes through my lungs so that I'm coughing instantly. I try to sit up but I can't. Something's trapping me. Jerking at my arms almost breaks them as they're tied so hard to what...the bed? I fall back and try to right my breathing, try to look around to see where I am.

The first thing I see are red eyes, then ice-blue ones. I know where I am and I know that I'm damned.

"Finally, you are awake," a raspy voice says but I've closed my eyes again. I don't want to see the fire and ice girls. Not until I'm ready for them.

"Let me see your eyes," the voice beckons. "Let me look into them while you read my mind."

Curiosity has me opening my eyes then because I want to know who this is that thinks they know me and my power and who was bold enough to kidnap me.

Never in my wildest dreams would I have imagined it would be him. Never, ever, ever. All the scenarios I'd given for how Dylan came to be were wrong. Everything I thought was wrong.

"You recognize me, I see." He chuckles. "The price I pay for being on television, huh."

"Walter Bryant," I whisper his name and my heart skips a beat. I'm speaking. I can hear myself speaking even though this is a fearful and confrontational situation. I'm speaking and I can be heard.

"And you remember my name. I'm flattered," he says, moving closer to the bed I'm tied to.

If believing that the guy I fell for was some instrument in this supernatural war was hard for me to swallow, accepting that I'm now being held captive in who knows what location is really blowing my mind. How did things get to this point? How did I, a diplomat's daughter living out her teenage years, end up here?

"Now let me see your eyes." He stands right above me now, his fingers touching right above my eyes, lifting so they'll open wider. "Remarkable how normal they look," he comments.

I squeeze my eyes shut, my fists balling at the sides. Bryant is a tall man, with a thin build. He has a light complexion, like coffee with lots of cream and his eyes are green, like the color of seawater. Wire-rim glasses sit on a long straight nose giving him an intellectual look. It's the webbed wrinkles in his cheeks as he smiles that make him look dangerous. Funny how I can easily recognize those traits now.

"You will give me what I want!" he yells. "All of you will give me exactly what I want."

My plan is to stay silent and uncooperative. But remaining quiet was never my strong point. "We're not giving you anything!" I scream right back. I've opened my eyes so I can see his lips spreading in that wide Joker-like grin. He looks nothing like he did when he was on television delivering the local weather. Nor does he look like a father, a small-town man with simple values and simple dreams. No, that's not the man I'm looking at now. His eyes are dancing around, fingers shaking just a touch as he rubs them over the scruffy hair growth at his chin and cheeks. Deranged would be a better word to describe what Walter Bryant looks like now.

"We'll just see about that." His hands fall from his face,

to rub together as he takes a step back. Isis and Ivy step forward. "Girls, do you think you could make her more cooperative?"

Of course I don't want whatever they can do to me, but then again, he's not asking what I want right now. Ivy comes closer to the bed, rubs a hand over my cheek and I swear it feels like every ounce of blood in my body freezes.

"Oh, I don't know. Her skin's so smooth. I'd just like to touch her for a while," she says, blowing a chilly breath over my face as she speaks.

I try to turn my head away from her but Isis is right on the other side. "Or I could touch her," she says, wiggling her fingers in front of my face, her eyes glistening with flames.

"Stop." His voice is low, level, familiar. "I can get what you need from her."

Ivy pauses, her fingers hovering over the line of my jaw. She and Isis both look away from me, toward him.

Dylan stands at the end of the bed. He's wearing what looks like a black jogging suit. His hair is slicked back and looks like he used about half a can of product to achieve this eerie kind of shine. His face looks harder, his jaw sharper and his gaze is connected inextricably with mine.

"You just want to make out with her some more," Isis spits toward him. Heat suddenly fills the side of the room she's on and I squirm on the bed uncomfortably.

Ivy moans, an eerie sound that makes me think of thunder for some reason. "Yeah, we didn't get to have any fun during this assignment."

"I said I can handle it," Dylan says, his voice rising a little higher.

He's still looking at me as I'm trying to figure this all out. The room is dim, all I can make out are walls with something scribbled on them. I can't really decipher what the something is except it looks like symbols or equations of some sort. There doesn't seem to be any furniture in here except for the bed I'm lying on. Bryant is standing near what I'm thinking is the only entrance and exit.

It's like a dream in here, or what I think a dream is supposed to look like. All grayscale-tinted and mysterious-feeling. Except all the eyes are colored, like a splash of paint on a dark canvas. Bryant's eyes, Ivy's and Isis's, even Dylan's. Like something is making them brighter, something not natural.

"Leave them," Bryant says, abruptly. "Five minutes and I'm coming back for her. She'll do what I tell her or she'll die. It's quite simple," he says with a curt nod that I presume is meant to bring the fire and ice twins with him.

With a surprisingly girlish pout, Ivy pulls her hand away from my face. I breathe a sigh of relief as my teeth finally stop chattering on that side of my mouth. Isis stands straight as she walks closer to Dylan.

"If you mess this up he's going to kill you, too, and possibly us. Keep that in mind when you're alone with her," she says to him.

"Remember, her time is limited no matter what you do," Isis adds.

twenty-two

Last Kiss

There's a loud click and I know that's Bryant locking us inside. I should feel fear bubbling inside of me. I should be speechless and wondering what the next step should be. Up until this point that's how I've always felt in frantic and stress-filled situations.

Tonight, however, I feel differently.

"So this was all an elaborate set-up," I say to Dylan, still watching him closely.

"He sent us here to do a job," he says as easily as if he's just given me the time of day.

"Who? Bryant? How does he know you? Where did you come from?"

There's a second when I don't think he's going to answer me, then his shoulders hang a little looser and I presume he's accepting both our fates now, figuring there's no harm in telling me the truth. I won't live long enough to use it, anyway. The words aren't there, but the undertone is like a livewire throughout the room.

"I'm from York, Pennsylvania. At least that's what I remember." He's talking quietly, almost like he doesn't want anyone to hear him, not even me.

"How did you end up here?" My question sits on the air for endless seconds, my mind turning as it does. Dylan is from out of town, just like I'm willing to bet everything I owned Ivy and Isis were, too. I'm not liking where this is going and I'm not even entirely sure I'm thinking along the right lines since I was so wrong before.

"He selected us. Something about our minds being prime for this sort of work."

"What were you supposed to do?"

"Seduce you," he answers simply.

I swallow because no way was I expecting that answer.

He rubs a hand over his hair and sighs. "Seduce you into relinquishing your power to him. That's all he wants, Lindsey. He just wants to know how you got this power so he can duplicate it or harvest it or whatever. All he said I had to do was to get you to read my mind and he'd have all the answers he needed."

Coincidentally, that's all Bryant needed and that's all I've been trying to do. But I never could read Dylan's mind. I was always blocked, now I have to wonder why.

Shaking my head isn't going to clear the disbelief. Especially since it's just like we figured. Project S is a study of the supernatural that Walter Bryant suspected was circling in Lincoln. His father had begun the research as a member of the Majestic 12 all those years ago. When he was supposed to be working for the government, protecting the inhabitants of Earth from extraterrestrial invasions, Jonathan Bryant was plotting a devious plan of his own. And now his son is trying to live out that legacy.

"He can't do that," I whisper, shock still reverberating in my head.

Dylan nods. "He can," he answers simply. "He did something to us. To me and to Isis and Ivy. We weren't like this before." He's looking at his hands now, wiggling his fingertips.

"You didn't have power. You weren't born with it?"

"No. I wasn't born a freak," he spits and looks at me angrily. "I was just heading into my senior year and there was this bus trip. We all wanted to go. A week away from our parents was going to be bliss. Who cared if we had to sing some hymns or read some scriptures, it was still a week away without their rules and regulations."

I sigh, because Dylan's just confirmed another one of my thoughts.

"That bus that went missing, you were on it. You and those girls. How did Bryant know about you?"

He shrugs. "I don't know all that. I'm not even supposed to remember as much as I do. That's why he sent the girls with me. They were supposed to keep me focused on doing the job."

The job of seducing me. I still can't believe that part. But I'm silent because there's so much going through my mind right now. So much we thought we knew, but really had no clue how deep it was.

"But I couldn't," Dylan whispers.

I look at him and he's walking closer to the bed, using his fingers to push hair away from my face. I should jerk away, resist his touch somehow, but I don't. I can't. For the first time since we met I feel something from Dylan, I feel a part of him.

"I watched you and I waited. When I thought the time was right, or rather when they thought I was taking too long, I got on that bus with you. Sitting behind you in class was like—" He stops, sighs. "I don't know what it was like. I don't remember ever feeling it before. I'm all confused about what's truth about my past and what's been engineered. And I hate what he's done to me!"

Dylan's jaw clenches, his eyes darkening with his rage.

"It wasn't supposed to be like this. I was supposed to finish out senior year, graduate, go to Texas on a football scholarship. Now that's all gone! It's all gone because of him!"

And he's more than pissed about it. I feel it now, pure and putrid, the rage that simmers inside Dylan at this very moment. It's directed at Walter Bryant, at whatever he'd done to them when he took them off that bus.

"There was one boy, they found him dead in the river," I say tentatively, not sure if Dylan wants to finish with his story but needing my own answers regardless.

"There were seven of us, along with Minister Hobbs. Three guys and four girls. We're the only ones alive," he says, giving me a pointed look. "The others didn't survive the experiment."

"How?" I can't help but ask.

"It's in the eyes. Windows to the soul, he said. And the soul holds the power."

I've heard "windows to the soul" before, Jake's grandfather told us that day before the tornado hit Lincoln. He'd been right all along. But how did Walter Bryant know about that?

"He wants your eyes to harvest the power you hold, to create more like you."

Swallowing is becoming harder and harder at the moment. "Where did he get the power he gave you and Isis and Ivy?"

Dylan shrugs. "I don't know who else he's working with but he talks to someone on his cell phone about stuff and he has these meetings late at night with somebody. I don't know any more than that."

And that is more than enough, I think. But I really need to get out of here to do something about it.

"You and me," I start to say even though I'd already sworn to myself not to go there. It was all a part of a plan, I get that. None of it was real. A cold hard fact, but one I'll learn to live with. No matter how much it stings.

Dylan looks at me fiercely. "We were real." He touches my hand. "Everything I said to you I meant. I knew what he wanted and I hesitated. Each time I was with you I hesitated. I couldn't just give you to him, couldn't lead you to…to…"

"To my death," I finish for him. No use clamming up now. "You didn't want to kill me."

He shakes his head.

I let out a nervous chuckle.

"And now?" I ask, my eyes focusing finally on the symbols on the wall around the room. I recognize some of them. "What do you want me to do now, Dylan? Give Bryant what he wants, give him my power? Then what? What happens to me and to you? Ivy and Isis?" Even though there's a big part of me that doesn't really care what happens to the evil twins. Still, I guess this isn't any more their fault than it was Dylan's. The person to blame is on the other side of that door.

"I can't help you," he says quietly.

"Can't or won't?"

When he turns to me again, staring at me, all the wind is knocked out of my chest and I gasp. Bright lights dance in front of my eyes, forming spectrums and spears of intense golden color. There's a thin mist of fog for a second before everything clears and I can see, finally, I can see.

Dylan's wearing a football uniform, white bottoms and a royal-blue shirt with the number 15 just beneath the name MURPHY. I know it's him even though his back is facing me. In one hand he holds a football, the other is clenched into a fist. Around him the all-too-familiar dark smoke swirls. The scene shifts and Dylan's facing me. His face as handsome as I remember without the fine edge of perfection. The hair is still dark, but not shining, his jawline is strong, but there's no dimple in his chin and his nose is just a little crooked. It's Dylan, but then it's not exactly. Except for the eyes, they're still blue, refreshing and poignant blue.

He wants peace, wants his simple life back but doesn't know how to get it. He's not evil. Not evil. I feel it. I know it. Dylan is not evil.

"Kiss me," I whisper, my eyes fluttering to stay open.

He looks perplexed.

"Dylan, I want you to kiss me," I say again, letting every muscle in my body relax, focusing my mind solely on Dylan. On kissing Dylan.

He takes a step forward, still not really sure that's what he should be doing. I keep focusing on him, being extremely careful not to break eye contact. It's inside me, what he's feeling, what he's thinking. It moves through me like a big puffy white cloud. There's goodness and laughter and fun, all of this is what Dylan really is. Who he was before…

And as he gets closer to me I keep looking, keep feeling. I can't lift my hands more than about five inches off the bed because of the restraints, but my left hand moves, reaches out to him. He doesn't even look down but lets his own fingers entwine with me. Heat rushes through each finger, up my arm to my shoulder, spreading like wildfire throughout the rest of my body.

"One last kiss," he whispers as he's lowering his face to mine.

I hope it won't be the last, but I can't see the future. All I see is right now, at this very moment. I'm watching Dylan, seeing all his innermost feelings, his deepest desires. He wants to kiss me. He wants to touch me. I want the same.

His name slips from my lips a millisecond before his lips touch me. Then I'm sinking, melting into the sweetness of our last kiss.

When I first met Dylan I never thought we'd have a first kiss, let alone a last one. Yet, I'm feeling it now, tasting how sweet things could have been between us had our circumstances been different. I love him, I know this with every fiber of my being. I love the Dylan Murphy he was.

My thoughts shift at that revelation. With our lips still intact I open my eyes. Here's another useless fact about kissing that doesn't seem so useless to me right now: As a rule, 66% of people keep their eyes closed while kissing. The rest take pleasure in watching the emotions race across the faces of their partners.

Dylan's eyes are still closed, his face tilted as the kiss deepens. He looks peaceful, feeling the bliss we both enjoyed about our kisses. He looks like this is where he wants to be and this is what he wants to be doing.

Until I change his mind.

Then he pulls back slowly. His eyelids flicker and finally open. I see his blue eyes that are now softer, kinder and his lips spread into a slow smile. He releases my fingers and moves his hands down to my wrist where he begins to undue the restraints. I don't move when both my hands are free but wait perfectly still while he works the bindings at my feet free.

His hands come to my waist and he lifts me off the bed until I'm standing directly in front of him. Lifting my hands I cup his face. "You are good, Dylan. You are very good," I say because I know the moment we break eye contact again he won't believe me. He'll be what Bryant created once again.

"You are good, Lindsey. Very, very good," is his reply.

"Time's up." Bryant's voice sounds through the door as he clicks the key into place.

"As soon as the door opens, you go. I'll take care of him," Dylan says.

I nod my head, watching with tremendous sadness as Dylan moves away from me to stand on one side of the door. I don't waste another moment on the feelings swelling up inside me. There's no time. I stand on the other side of the door waiting. As soon as it swings open Dylan jumps on Bryant. I don't look back but run through the door as fast as I can.

There's a long hall and of course it's dark. I don't know where I'm going. Don't have a clue but I keep running. I hear footsteps behind me but don't chance a look back. As long as I'm not bumping into any walls I'm going to keep running. In the distance there's a slight glimmer of something but I swear this feels like the longest run in the longest hallway I've ever taken. I wonder where I am but don't have time to figure it out.

Behind me there's a blast of heat and I know that Isis is back there and she's gaining fast. My heart hammers in my chest and I feel like I'm back by the water, running through the forest toward something that calls to me. Keep running, keep running, it's like a mantra in my head. Then suddenly, the glimmer I saw in the distance shatters. I realize when tiny flecks smack into my face painfully that the glimmer was glass and it's now breaking into thousands of tiny pieces.

There's a loud screeching sound, one like I've never heard before. It stings my ears threatening to break my stride but I keep going. In front of me it's coming. I see it but don't know what "it" is. This feeling inside of me pushes me forward, regardless, so I keep running. Then something sharp catches my shoulder and my legs are moving but my feet are no longer touching the floor.

Wind slaps against my face, stinging the parts that were nicked by the glass. I open my mouth and this time a scream wails into what I see is now the night air. Below is the football field, the broken and burnt scoreboard still lying on the far end where it fell after Dylan struck it down.

They were holding me in the school. And now, now, I'm flying through the air, or more like dangling from. When I look up I scream again. It's a huge bird and it's carrying me through the air. I'm gripped tightly in its talon so even though I keep squirming I'm probably not going to fall. And just when I think either my heart's going to thump right out of my chest or I'm going to embarrass myself in some other distasteful way, I see the bird's face.

Ever hear the phrase, "she never saw it coming?" Well imagine that to the kazillionth power.

twenty-three

The Guardians

I don't fall out of the sky and break both my legs, which I guess could have been a possibility. Instead, I'm dropped to the ground with a light thump. For a few seconds I just lie there trying to get my thoughts together. It doesn't work. So much has happened tonight, so many revelations I feel like my head is literally spinning with all this information.

Wings flap behind me. I hear them and I'm afraid to turn around.

"Look at me, Lindsey."

No. No. No. I chant to myself. I'm face-first on the ground, smelling the grass like it's some kind of stimulant.

"You cannot hide from what is. This is who I really am. I am your Guardian."

I hear her and it sounds just like Mrs. Hampton. When I saw that bird's face it looked just like Mrs. Hampton. So why am I shaking my head refusing to believe that Mrs. Hampton has shifted into some type of creature?

"The longer you stay there the longer I will be this way. We don't have a lot of time."

It's that stern coolness in her voice that finally has me

moving. In all the time I've lived with Mrs. Hampton she's been stern with me, but she's taken good care of me. Never has she said or done anything to harm me. And considering what she just saved me from, I guess I don't have to worry about that happening now.

Rolling over slowly I sit up and can do nothing but stare. She's huge and she's a bird with a human face.

"What are you?" I finally manage to croak.

"I am a harpy."

It takes me a second longer than usual because it's late, I've been almost frozen, almost burned and swooped out a window, I'm not a hundred percent on point at the moment. "Winged spirits who stole from Phineas." I finally recall the Greek mythological definition of a harpy.

She nods. Her graying hair is flowing long and curly and lies against a dull black layer of feathers that go all the way down her broad back and fan into two huge wings. Sharp talons dig up the grass as she moves about the backyard. She's almost as big as the house and I'm not making a joke. No wonder she has all this space and lives here alone. She couldn't fit anywhere else.

"I don't understand."

Her head nods. "We didn't think you would, that's why we didn't tell you. It does not matter at the moment. There is much to be done and not a lot of time."

I'm already shaking my head. "Are all Guardians like you?"

"Not exactly."

"But you each know about one another?"

"Yes."

"And my parents knew," I add, remembering the dream

I had before waking to see the fire and ice twins. "My mother gave me that spell, the same one you said that night by the water." The feeling of fog clearing from my mind is a relief as I manage to stand and brush the grass off my legs.

"Both of your parents knew what you were as well as what would one day come for you. They were very proud of you and your purpose. You know that, don't you?"

I didn't know, not until this last dream. The way they'd both looked at me right after the crash. Their eyes said it all—they knew, they cared, they supported me. Their dying eyes said they loved me and my throat clogs with emotion.

"I can fight him now," I say between trembling lips.

Mrs. Hampton nods. "I know you can. Now let's get you cleaned up."

Before I can turn toward the house the harpy shrinks, those huge wings slipping into beefy human arms, talons fitting back into furry bedroom slippers. All the long curly hair rolls itself right back into that tight bun I'm used to seeing. It's a seamless transition that takes all of two seconds and looks as natural as summer rain. My breath only hitches a little this time, then picks up a steady pace as Mrs. Hampton walks to me and puts an arm around my shoulder. We walk into the house together and she leads me to the bathroom to clean the small cuts on my face. We don't talk during this time but I swear we're closer now than we've been in the entire year I've lived here. And moving to my room to change my clothes I feel like maybe, finally, I might really be home.

twenty-four

Game Over

"We're at the field. You need to get here fast," is all Jake says before the call is disconnected.

I'd just changed into clean clothes and was heading down the steps to go and see the others when my cell phone rang. Now I'm at the door when Mrs. Hampton throws me a set of keys.

"Take my car, it'll be faster."

"You're not coming?" I ask almost afraid to think of going out without her, which is crazy since a few hours ago I was climbing out of my window without telling her.

She shakes her head. "We are there when we are needed."

"But how will you know?"

Her hand is on my shoulder again pushing me toward the door. "You go do your job and I will do mine," she tells me.

I don't ask any more questions but slip out the door and run to her late-model Nissan. As I drive my ankle starts to heat and know that the mark there is glowing. Power soars through my body and I feel more alive at this very moment than I ever have. I have no idea what I'm walking into. I know what I left at the school so I can probably guess, but now my friends are there. Adrenaline shoots a slow buzz through my system and I press down harder on the gas, in a hurry to get there.

Walter Bryant is not in his right mind but a part of me has to give him credit for being good enough to take an ordinary human and give them supernatural powers. I don't wish death on anybody but I sure am glad that there were only three to survive that religious retreat. I don't know if we could take on more than that of these powerful hybrids.

Then again, I think we could. Four powers together are much stronger than one. We can do anything, that's why she chose us. I believe that now with all my being. I believe that we have a purpose and that we will prevail.

If I could ever get to the school.

When I arrive at the field it's complete chaos. Fire is spewing from most of the school's windows while the gate separating the field's perimeter from the line of trees leading into the forest is covered in ice. From the distance I can see that the grass in the center of the field has been burned. I think it may be in some sort of symbol but I can't tell from this far away.

Just as I'm about to take off running across the field I'm grabbed by the back of my shirt and pulled down behind a car.

"What the—"

"Shh," Krystal says, putting a hand over my mouth.

"I don't know why we're whispering, they want us to see what they're doing. They want somebody to see, that's for sure," Sasha quips.

"We still have the element of surprise," Krystal replies, letting her hand fall from my lips when I nod in agreement.

"We came looking for you and this is what we found," Jake says, nodding his head toward the school. "At first we thought you were trapped inside but then Krystal said you weren't, so we texted you."

"I was here earlier but Dylan helped me escape. You're never going to believe who's orchestrating this."

"I saw your boyfriend over by the back door," Sasha says.

Her voice doesn't have that tone it did before when she talked about Dylan, she's just stating a fact. One she wants to be sure I know.

I nod. "He was here when I left. With the fire and ice twins and with Walter Bryant."

"What?" Krystal's trying to whisper so the word comes out more like a hiss than a question.

"How does Bryant know Dylan and the twins?" Jake asks.

I know they're not going to like this and for the first time I think of Sasha's secondary connection to this situation. Her father knew about Project S, was helping Bryant to fund it. And if that was the case…

"Bryant's Project S created Dylan and the twins. They were on the bus that went missing from the religious retreat. Bryant used them all as lab rats, experimenting on them to see if he could actually create supernaturals himself."

"No way," Jake says then frowns. "I don't want to believe it, but I know it's true."

"I thought Charon had sent Dylan. I thought they were all demons," Sasha says quietly. She's thinking about her father's connection just like I am.

I don't plan to bring it up if she doesn't, though. Because, let's face it, she's been through enough already.

"He really created supernaturals?" Krystal still can't believe it. "I wonder how he did it."

"I don't care how. I just want them all gone," Jake declares.

"We can't just kill them," she protests.

"What are our other options? Call the cops and have those twins burn or freeze them to death? I don't even want to think of the damage Dylan can do if provoked. They need to go. Now!" His voice gets louder and the car we're hiding behind shakes with the vibration.

"How do we get rid of them?" Sasha asks.

She's trying to be brave, to get this over with because her heart is heavy with guilt. Her father is involved in this and thus she thinks she's partially responsible. I wish I had time to convince her how wrong she is. But blue streaks of lightning soar into the air, ripping through the sky with an eerie crackle.

"It doesn't even look like natural lightning," Krystal says, looking up.

"No. It doesn't," I add, my own heart a little heavy at the sight. That's Dylan out there, the Dylan I love and the Dylan I'll never have.

Jake stands up a little and peers through one of the windows of the car. "They're all out there now, standing in the center of the field. They want someone to see them, to know about their power."

"You think they did all this just to get us here?" Krystal asks.

"No. They want the world to know they're here," I tell

them. "Bryant wanted me to give him my power. He wants to harvest it so he can implant it into another human."

"Creating more supernaturals," Sasha finishes.

"Right. Dylan was supposed to let me read his mind then I guess my powers would transfer to him or he could detract them from me for Bryant. I don't know how it works specifically, all I know is that in the end, Dylan didn't do it. He didn't go through with the plan." They didn't need to know why he didn't go through with it—because I influenced his mind to do something different.

Sasha rubs a hand over her face and takes a deep breath. "What happened to the others from the bus?"

"They're dead," I answer solemnly.

"Jeez," Krystal whispers. "This is nuts. Bryant is nuts!"

"I agree," Jake adds. "So here's what we're going to do. We need a diversion, something to get their attention while I sneak up from behind. If I can catch them off guard maybe I can do some damage before they have a chance to strike back."

It's as good a plan as any considering Jake has the most active power, but I'm not so sure I like the idea of Dylan being damaged. I know, it's silly, this is the situation and I need to deal with it. But I can deal with it in my own way.

"I can get their attention," Sasha says, standing.

"Good. I'll go around back," Jake says before hunching behind other cars then breaking into a run at the corner where the parking lot opens up.

"What are you going to do?" Krystal asks Sasha.

"I'm going to make them think they're seeing things. You two stay here and watch me," she says.

In the next instant Sasha's body goes lax against the car.

Krystal and I lower her to a sitting position and crouch, still high enough so we can look through the window to the field. What we see has us both gasping. Ivy is shooting ice into the sky, Isis aims directly at the ice so that it comes back down as a misty rain over the field only. Through the mist Dylan's blue lightning cracks and sizzles. Bryant stands behind them watching with arms folded over his chest like the ever-proud parent.

Right in front of them Sasha appears with her hands on her hips. "Hey!" she yells.

Bryant looks at her and smiles. "Welcome to the party, Miss Carrington. It's been a great pleasure working with your father. He's told me so much about you."

"I'll just bet he has," Sasha quips with her signature smile. "So what are you doing out here? Performing, like the circus?" She laughs at her own joke.

Behind the car Krystal and I chuckle, too.

Ivy acts first, directing her icy glare at Sasha in an attempt to freeze her, but Sasha disappears, moving to stand right beside Isis, who she taps on the shoulder.

"You should tell her to chill out," she says.

Then Isis turns, opens her mouth and breathes fire like a dragon out of a storybook. Sasha's gone before the flames can even touch the illusion of her body. She reappears behind Bryant this time.

"My father really needs to listen to his financial advisors more often. Backing your bogus project is going to ruin him," she says.

"Not before I kill you!" Bryant turns fast, his arms outstretched in an attempt to grab Sasha but he falls right through the illusion and slams into the ground.

Beside us Sasha's body jerks and she lifts her head laughing. Krystal and I laugh right along with her, pumped at how cool it was to watch her moving all over, confusing them. Then there's a deafening crash and we all jump up. Jake's standing at the doors to the school, the fire and ice twins and Dylan are across the field on their knees, while Walter Bryant is kneeling in front of Jake.

"Stop! Stop!" he yells, his hands up in the air like Jake's a cop.

We break out running across the field. I immediately go to Jake's side looking at Bryant. His glasses are cracked and hanging off one side of his face. He's afraid of Jake, afraid of what he might do to him. But he's still thinking he can get out of this.

"He's trying to come up with a plan," I tell Jake who just frowns.

"Whatever it is, it won't work," Jake says, grabbing Bryant by the collar and lifting him up off the ground. "You messed up big-time, weatherman."

Before I can protest—and I don't really know that I would have—Jake throws Bryant all the way across the field.

"They're coming!" Sasha screams, pointing at Dylan and the twins, who are quickly making their way back to us.

Jake steps away from us. "Get behind me!" he yells.

We hurry over by the annex building that's part of the gym and stand behind him. Just as Dylan and the twins get close to the building, Jake pushes against the bricks.

"No!" I scream instinctively and feel Krystal pulling me back because I must have jumped up at the same time.

Jake pushes against the building and it begins to crumble.

Glass and brick and drywall and furniture all tumble down, covering the twins. And Dylan.

I can't breathe, can't see beyond the dust from the rubble, but mostly I just can't breathe. "No," I whisper, sinking to my knees. My hands fall to the grass, nails digging in the dirt. "No."

"He had to do it, Lindsey. There was no other way," I hear Krystal saying from one side.

Tears sting my eyes and burn my throat. I cough a little then let them flow. They burn my cheeks and fill my heart with even more sadness, more grief. I want to scream with agony but I don't. This had to happen, it had to be in order for us to survive. That doesn't lessen the sting or the evil burden of grief. This time, it exemplifies it.

Sasha hugs me to her and we rock back and forth, right there on the field.

"I know honey, I know," she says over and over again.

I feel comforted by Sasha. Not that I wasn't by Krystal. But it's different with Sasha, it's different now. We're connected by something more than our powers. It's sad and gut-wrenching, but it's true. We're connected by two senseless deaths that leave us both with broken hearts.

In the morning I'm awakened by my cell phone ringing repeatedly. I've heard it for a while now but was hoping it was in my dreams. When I came home last night Mrs. Hampton took one look at me and said I'd had a rough day—that was an understatement. I didn't ask her if she knew what happened at the school. I already knew she did. Anyway, it had already been decided that I wouldn't be going to school today, and from the looks of the building when I left there last night, neither would anyone else. So who is this calling me when it's still too early to think about getting up?

Figuring the answer to that question would only come if I picked up the phone, I slap my hand on the nightstand and scoop it up.

"Hello," is what I mean to say but it comes out like some muffled jargon.

"Jake's on his way to get you. It's Sasha, she's in trouble," Krystal says before hanging up.

I'm up out of the bed as if I weren't just dead-to-the-world asleep a few minutes ago. With the world's record for the shortest wash-up, I fly through the bathroom and back into my room to grab something to put on. I'm heading down the steps when Mrs. Hampton stops me right at the bottom.

"This is a different kind of power you will face. Be extra careful," she says all *Mission Impossible* crypticlike.

I don't wait to try and figure it out, just head for the door just in time to see Jake pulling up. Like I said it's too early because the sun is barely up and it still smells fresh out here. I climb into the truck and ask immediately, "What's going on?"

He shrugs. "Krystal got a vision of Sasha surrounded by flames and told me to come get you and meet at Sasha's house."

"You think it's her dad?"

"I hope not."

"I don't think Bryant died in that rubble," I say because as I'd fallen asleep last night, I remember Jake throwing him across the field but I didn't remember seeing Bryant come back. He would have been too far away for the annex building collapse for any of it to have touched him.

"Me, either."

We're quiet the rest of the ride and pull up in front of Sasha's front door just in time to see Walter Bryant tumbling through the front door and Mouse standing there watching him roll down the front steps.

twenty-five

Madness

Jake is out of the car and running and I follow behind him. He grabs Bryant up holding him so the man's feet are off the ground.

"What did you do to her? What did you do?"

He's shaking Bryant who already looks like he's been beat up.

"Nothing." Bryant coughs. "Nothing."

"Where is she?"

"I don't know. I don't know." Bryant crumples to the ground when Jake drops him. "It's Carrington, he's gone crazy," he says, spitting blood onto the pristine concrete.

Mrs. Carrington is not going to like that.

"He's going to kill her! For real he's going to kill her!"

Jake and I don't waste another moment on Bryant but run into the house. It's pandemonium in here with the two new young housekeepers huddled in a corner, hugging each other and crying. They're saying something in Spanish but they're crying so hard I can't understand them.

It sounds like the roof is about to cave in and Jake and I run up the stairs. Mrs. Carrington is sitting in a corner at the far end of the hall. All the carpet in this house is a very light beige color so any stain shows up as if it was Lite-Brite. Blood is no exception. She's bleeding from a wound to her head and I feel that familiar pang in my temple.

"Go see how she is. I'll find Sasha," Jake directs me.

I hurry down the hallway.

"Hi, Mrs. Carrington," I say softly, going to my knees. "Can you stand up? We can go downstairs and I'll call 911."

She shakes her head, her long dark hair—so much like Sasha's—is matted to one side of her face and sticking up on the other.

"Too late," she whispers and her voice sounds hoarse.

I lower my ear closer to her mouth because she's trying to say something else but it's so low I barely hear her. "He wants her dead. She cost him money so he wants her dead."

"Who?" I ask even though I know exactly who she's talking about.

"I don't understand," she continues. "She's his child and she's just a baby."

"Okay," I say, touching the side of her face. "It's okay, we won't let anything happen to her."

Then I stand leaving her there because I want to find Jake and Sasha. And where's Krystal?

I head to the other side of the floor because that's where I hear the most noise and when I step inside, it's to see Jake fighting with Mr. Carrington. They're rolling on the floor, the two of them, and I pause a beat before I figure out what to do. Going to get one of the chairs that sits at a desk I lift it into the air and wait until Mr. Carrington is closest to me then bring the chair crashing down on his back. He yells and lets go of Jake who stands quickly.

"We need to find Sasha! Check downstairs!"

I run out of the room with Jake right behind me. I feel like I'm flying down the twisting stairs and going through the house room by room until we get to her father's office. Krystal is at the door looking at something neither Jake nor I see. With a nod of her head she opens the door to the office. I don't know if she saw us or not but we step into the office behind her. Sasha's sitting in the center of her father's desk, her hair is wild, tears streaking her face, a bruise on her left arm.

She's hurt and she's afraid and above all else she's tired. Her entire body is wilting under all the pressure she's been under with her parents and the Mystyx and losing Twan, it's all closing in on her and she's feeling like now might just be the time to let go of it all.

We walk to her slowly. Krystal touches her first, hugging her close. "Come on, honey, let's get you out of here."

But Sasha doesn't move. I knew she wouldn't. "The police are already on their way. I called 911. All we have to do is get out of this house and you won't ever have to come back." I tell her this and I mean it. I'll ask Mrs. Hampton to take custody of Sasha if need be, but I won't be able to sleep another night knowing she's with these whack jobs that call themselves parents.

"I don't have anywhere to go. This is where I belong," she says in a soft voice that is so unlike Sasha I want to scream.

"That's it!" Jake yells. "You're coming with us." He pushes Krystal to the side and lifts Sasha up off the desk.

We all turn to leave and are greeted by huge flames bursting through the door.

Jake curses and Krystal gasps. Me, I'm so sick of seeing fire I don't know whether to cry or scream. Instead, I head for the windows and pick up another chair tossing it right through the opening. If Mrs. Carrington were in here she'd have a heart attack at the way I've been treating her furniture.

Everybody moves closer to the window and we're about to start filing out when the wall behind us opens up and through the opening comes a maniacal-looking Mr. Carrington.

"You stupid kids! Do you know how much money you've cost me? Stupid, stupid freak kids!" he yells.

He has a gun and is pointing it directly at Jake and Sasha.

The moment freezes, like in the movies, everybody just goes instantly still. In the distance I hear footsteps, smell the smoke from the fire then all I see is debris flying everywhere.

It didn't come through an opening in the wall like Mr. Carrington, it made its own opening. I don't know what it is exactly but it aims directly for Mr. Carrington, grabbing him by the midsection and lifting him to the air. My head follows his body as I watch him being shaken to death. It's a gruesome sight but I'm so amazed by what's doing this to him that I can't tear my gaze away.

"You must leave this place right now, Jake."

I know that voice. And it does avert my attention from Mr. Carrington.

It's Jake's grandfather.

But it's not.

I mean, I'm not real surprised seeing what I see because I've already seen Mrs. Hampton in her other form. Still, it's not every day in the twenty-first century a girl would look a black-winged horse eye to eye.

Jake turns at the sound of the voice, looks at the Pegasus and doesn't move. Coming through the opening is a huge snake's head and I take a step back figuring this is Krystal's Guardian.

"We should leave now, explain later," Jake's grandfather says again.

"Right," Jake says, stumbling only for a second.

Around me I hear boards creaking and crashing down. Smoke begins to fill my lungs and for a minute I'm thrust back into that train the day it crashed. With one hand to my stomach and the other to my forehead I sway and try to focus. Someone's calling my name and I swear it's my mother. But it's not.

"Lindsey, let's go!"

It's Mrs. Hampton. I hear the flapping of her huge wings just outside the house that as I look around is not much of a house anymore. I start to jump over the debris making my way to the hole in the wall when I glance over and see Sasha's father's body. It's not a nice sight and yet it gives me great relief to know he won't be working with Bryant to harvest our powers.

Outside it's something straight out of a storybook. Jake and Krystal are on the back of Mr. Kramer—the black Pegasus. Sasha's limp body is thrown over the back of an animal or a combination of different animals that I think is Casietta. Mrs. Hampton stands right next to me in all her harpy glory and the huge python—I can identify the type of reptile now that I'm a little closer to it—stands on her other side.

Hearing sirens in the distance I slip onto Mrs. Hampton's back and let her whisk me away.

Looking down as we go, I sigh. It's not every day a girl watches her best friend's house being burned to the ground with her parents still in it. Just like it wasn't every day a girl held her own parents' hands and watched them die. Different circumstances, same results. Sasha was going to be a mess for months. I plan to be there for her, helping her try to get through. It won't be easy, I know this from experience. At least, she won't be alone.

twenty-six

The Beginning of The End

"They have failed," Lor says in a thick gravely voice.

From his throne Charon sits, two large ravens with bloodred eyes flanking his sides. "I am not surprised."

He never believed the humans would be able to assist him in this battle. Both of them were weak and filled with greed. Approaching them had been like a game to see how fast they would self-destruct. This was just another reason Charon felt he was superior to the mortals. They were not on his level; even when he gave them help they could not do his simple bidding.

This war would have to be won by him just as he knew would always be the way. It would come down to him and Styx once again. And this time he planned to walk away the victor.

"Together they are powerful."

Frowning, Charon waved a robed hand at Lor. The dark demon was beginning to bother him, just as this entire ordeal was. All he ever wanted was to take his rightful place, to achieve his destiny. She shouldn't have stopped him, shouldn't have tried to deny him. Letting his head fall back against the chair and his skeletal fingers grip the sides, he began the chant, the call to battle, the rise of his minions.

Lor began to laugh, that sick ugly sound that echoed off the blue-black walls of the Underworld. As his body filled with power his mind looked to the future and could hardly wait. They were coming to them, all of his creations to do his bidding. They would end this once and for all. The beginning was done. The end is here.

"There's an eclipse tonight," I say as we sit on the grass surrounding the grave of Jake's grandfather.

I hate that we're here, in the cemetery again. But it just seems like people keep dying. First Jake's grandfather, then Twan, now Sasha's parents and Walter Bryant. While I can't say I'm all that sorry about Sasha's dad and Bryant, I'm just getting a little sick of death.

It makes me think about my own mortality, about how long I'll have and what I'll do with the time. I used to think that life was endless—of course I was like four when I thought that. Still, I figured I had time to do all the things I wanted to do when I wanted to do them. Now, I know differently.

There were things I know my parents still wanted to do, like see me graduate from high school and move on to college and then my career. My father wanted to buy a vacation home in Hawaii and mom was going to grow peanuts or pineapples or something there. They'd planned to grow old together, to live out their golden years happily. Now they were gone.

Swallowing the grief and commanding it to stay down I

don't cry as I sit staring at all the headstones around me. Instead, I look at them, reading the names, vowing to avenge each senseless death. In that vow I dedicate myself to fighting this battle with Charon once and for all and know that tonight will be the night.

"I heard the news this morning. It's at eight o'clock tonight," Krystal says.

She's normally really quiet in the cemetery. I guess because so many of her spirits come to her here. Today she seems more apt to talk, even to move around.

Sasha on the other hand is really quiet. She stayed with me at Mrs. Hampton's last night where she fell into a quick, deep sleep. This morning we didn't talk a lot. She looked like she wanted to be alone, so I let her be. This wasn't going to be easy for her, no matter how much she disliked her father. Knowing that we'd had a hand in his death was not going to be the highlight of the summer before her senior year.

The fact that her mother's and Mr. Bryant's bodies were burned in the fire, too, was going to be an issue as well. The local news had covered the story at length since Bryant was one of theirs. If they only knew the real person he was. They'd also mentioned Franklin, a name none of us had dared say in months.

I really wish there was something more I could do for Sasha. I know what it feels like to grieve and to hurt so much you think your next breath is going to kill you, too. I don't envy her that feeling at all.

I miss Dylan that way. Even though in my mind I knew there would only be one option for him, it doesn't make knowing that he's gone any easier.

Jake's rubbing his fingers over the letters of his grandfather's stone.

"I still can't believe it," he's saying. "What they all turned into, how they came to our defense. It was unbelievable."

I nod. "Yeah, it was. It was good to see Casietta again, right Sasha?" Later last night, I learned that Casietta's other form was that of a chimera.

With both hands Sasha slips her hair back behind her ears and nods in answer. "I knew she was still alive, even if it's on another plane."

The Guardians' first home is the Majestic, that's where they can live in their natural forms. They're allowed in this realm to protect us. Upon their death from the earthly realm they offer protection by watching from the Majestic and appearing in their natural form when needed.

"I still can't believe Gerald has been my Guardian all this time, and a python, as well. He's always acted like he hates me," Krystal says.

I shrug. "He didn't act that way last night."

"No, he didn't," she says with a sigh. "My mother said that's why she came back to Lincoln and married him. She'd run to New York with my dad hoping to escape my destiny, but in the end she knew she'd have to bring me back. Now she's hoping her faith can help hold the balance of good and evil steady. Once we get rid of Charon, I mean."

And that last sentence renders us all silent.

"It will be tonight," Jake says finally as he turns to us.

I nod.

Sasha sighs. "It will be the end," she speaks quietly.

"We will prevail," Krystal says and stands up moving

around Jake's grandfather's headstone and down a small slope.

Each of us looks at the other but it's Jake who starts to follow her first. Something about the way Krystal's voice changed had me standing and following, too. I hear Sasha behind me although her steps are slower.

When she stops at the grave of Ricky Watson, I sigh. Ricky was the first ghost Krystal willingly listened to. They have a special bond I think, even though I don't really know how you could bond with a ghost. I guess if I were a medium I could. Instead, I'm just an empath who bonded with a hybrid demon. We make some team here.

Krystal's arm reaches out in front of her and her hand moves as if she's touching something. She smiles and then turns to us.

"Ricky said hello," she announces.

Jake shifts uncomfortably and I just give her a small smile. Am I supposed to say hello to a ghost that I don't even see? Sasha doesn't said anything but turns away. Twan's headstone is right next to Ricky's since they were brothers. His grandmother already left Lincoln, giving Sasha her phone number to call her at any time. Sasha doesn't want to see either one of the graves and I can't really say I blame her. Dylan's grave wouldn't be here in Lincoln so I don't have to worry about running into it here, today.

"Sasha," Krystal calls her name as she walks over to her and takes her hand. "Twan has a message for you."

Sasha shakes her head so hard her hair falls around her face. Krystal continues to rub her hand. "He said he's fine and he's happy to be with his brother again."

Sasha hiccups as her soul fights over whether she should

be happy to hear from Twan or even more sad that he's not here with her.

"He said we have to do this tonight. We have to take care of Charon once and for all," Krystal continues.

"I can't," Sasha wails. "I can't."

"You can," Krystal insists.

I move to Sasha's side and take her other hand. "We all can and we will."

Jake joins us, taking my hand and Krystal's, making the circle complete. "We will, Sasha. Finally we will take care of this."

"A solar eclipse occurs when the moon passes between the sun and the Earth. This can only happen during a New Moon, when the sun and moon are in conjunction as seen from the Earth. There are four types of eclipses: total, annual, partial and hybrid. During a total solar eclipse the moon completely covers the sun from the Earth's view, giving a general appearance of a ring of light in the darkened sky. That ring of light is called the solar corona. And from that ring of light, the Mystyx are born," Fatima speaks in her melodious voice, bringing us one last message.

I hear her words and think back. According to the calendars of the total solar eclipse, we're not slated to get one this year and the next one that will be visible from Earth will only be seen by those in Australia or on the Pacific Ocean. There's been special newscasts all day and evening because scientists were amazed to see their charts change and hurried to predict tonight's event, even though it's not likely that it will be visible from Earth.

Not to those who are not magicals, anyway.

But as we walk through the path in the woods where Sasha had driven us before and we'd seen the markings on the tree, we all know we'll be able to see the eclipse, just as we'll be able to see what comes with it.

"The eclipse completely closes off all light so the portals to all realms will be open. Charon will be able to walk on Earth," Fatima says.

"That's just great," Sasha quips and steps around a hanging branch.

Her mood is still off and we're all paying special attention to her. We need her to be ready and on point when the time comes. Right about now, I don't personally think she'll let us down. But I know Jake is skeptical. Krystal's hopeful but not really sure. I know that at the end of the day Sasha just wants all of this to be over. Just like I do.

Only Fatima's voice is with us, which seems a little eerie as we move through the dark forest with its inhabitants doing their nightly calls all around us. It seems kind of strange to be walking into a battle like this. I mean, we're just teenagers, not soldiers. We don't have any weapons, only the power given to us by a Greek goddess. That by itself is a lot to swallow.

And I'm a little worried that Mrs. Hampton wasn't at the house when I left. She never goes anywhere, that's reason number one I'm concerned. The fact that tonight's our final battle makes me wonder even more about her whereabouts. But there's no time for my mind to be anyplace else but here.

There's a very good chance that we won't be successful tonight. And if so, we can be assured a fate similar to Dylan and the fire and ice twins. I'm not really looking forward to that.

To keep my mind on more positive things I look up and see the sun looks like a half moon. It's weird because I'm not used to seeing the golden orb split this way. It's looming over the top of the trees kind of like a spaceship. I'm in the back of the line, Jake's up front, with Krystal behind him and Sasha in front of me. We're walking with a purpose but not really with a plan. That's backward, I know, but after being at the cemetery earlier today we all just wanted some time alone. We agreed to meet up here again tonight but hadn't talked to each other since. I don't think I would have had a lot to talk about, anyway.

"This is ridiculous," Sasha finally says and stops walking. "It's like we have a standing date and we're heading off to rendezvous. This is not a social call!" She crosses her arms over her chest and leans against the nearest tree.

Up ahead Krystal and Jake stop and turn around. Jake is thinking he knew this was going to happen. Krystal's wondering what we can do to stop it. Me, I think Sasha has a valid point.

"You know I was wondering myself how we know tonight is the night." I stand beside Sasha. "Shouldn't we feel something in particular? Like dread or anticipation."

"Are you two serious?" Jake asks through clenched teeth. "This is the moment we've been waiting for."

"Is it?" I propose. "How do we know for sure?"

"Fatima just told us and it seems right," Krystal says.

"But there's nobody here," Sasha adds. "It's just us walking around in this dark forest like we're off to see the wizard or something."

Her mood is definitely declining.

"This is serious," Jake says.

"We know that, Jake. But we're allowed to have questions and reservations. We don't have to walk just because you said walk," I add.

"That's not fair. We're in this together," Krystal says, defending Jake.

The atmosphere has changed. The once-quiet evening has turned chilly with a brisk wind rustling the leaves on the trees.

"What if they're wrong? What if it's not tonight? What if it's not here?" Sasha questions. "For all we know if he can walk the Earth tonight, what's stopping him from going anywhere else in the world? Why here? Why now? Why us?"

Her voice is a sickening wail on the wind and the answer is a ferocious roar of thunder and golden lightning bolts that crack through the dark sky.

That definitely gets all our attention as we shut our mouths simultaneously. Sasha lifts up from the tree. Krystal takes a step closer to Jake. And I, I feel the pounding of footsteps from behind, feel them with every thump of my heart. So when I turn around and barely see the shadowy silhouettes moving between the trees I don't even wait to try and decipher who or what they are. "Run!" I yell.

The others don't take long to join me as we rip through the trees, our feet crunching broken branches and debris. We run until we come to a sliding halt at the clearing where the tree is. It stands big and wide, much bigger than I remember it before. And the symbols on it are glowing white. There is no mistake now that this is the night and this is the place.

Thoughts of death and despair seep into my head and I stumble back at the intensity.

"He's here," I whisper when the darkness is clouding so much of my mind I feel sick to my stomach.

"I see him," Sasha says.

"He's summoned the souls of the dead, the ones who were awaiting transport to the Underworld. They're surrounding us."

And that's just how it feels, like we're being enclosed upon. The air is thick with evil, the cool breeze turning chilly enough to make me shiver.

Then the ground shakes and we all move to a tree to take hold thinking it's an earthquake. Trees sway and bend with the weight of the wind. They begin to crack as the rumbling seems more intense, closer, I think.

"The creature is coming," Sasha says.

My heart picks up pace because I'm remembering the time I was in the forest running from the creature. Steeling myself, I let go of the tree and clench my fists at my sides. It's showtime.

twenty-seven

The Darkness Cometh

Red eyes, that's what I see first breaking through the trees and the dark of night. Its actual body hasn't come into view yet, but I don't need to see it to know that it's huge and deadly. All I need to do is to keep my eyes on its.

Beside me, Jake is using his telekinesis to push the demon shadows back. Krystal seems to be chanting something, I'm not sure. I step out farther into the openness of the clearing so that I'm in direct line of sight of the creature. Even though I know he'll seek me out no matter where I go. My body jolts with each step it takes because the ground shakes, but I don't fall. I don't even waver anymore, I'm poised and ready. My neck is craned so that I can watch the tall creature as it's making its way toward me. I see his eyes but he hasn't looked at me yet. I need him to look at me.

As if sensing this dilemma Sasha appears right beside me. In the next instant she teleports to the other side of the clearing. She keeps doing this back and forth until the creature's gaze finally lands on mine. I feel the connection with a jolt and have to steady myself once more to keep the link.

It's beyond dark and angry, a swirling pit of black hatred and vengeance lives in its mind. I'm there now, among the fury and my body trembles, I don't know if I can stand it in here much longer. It's closer now, enough so that I can see its large scaly body. This is the same beast from that night at the club. I remember its face now, it matches the face of the smoke creature that had chased me at school. They are one and the same and its name is Lor. That's what Mouse told us. It's reportedly too ugly to show its real form in the earthly realm and thus the smoke figures. Tonight, however, those rules obviously do not apply.

With a crash of trees Lor busts through and stands partially in the clearing. Lifting its arms it roars again. It wants to look away, to rear back its head to show its true dominance but it can't. I have him locked in this gaze.

My ankle is on fire as power pours into me. Everything from my toenails to my eyelids feel invigorated, empowered. I can do this. I know I can.

"Go home." I say it in my mind first.

The creature roars again.

"Go home." This time I say it out loud.

The wind picks up, my hair wraps around my face, but I don't close my eyes. My entire body shakes. Around me I hear noises, voices, thoughts and sounds. I feel like I'm in motion but I know I'm standing still.

It's staring at me, baring its sharp teeth with all that yucky mucus dripping from them. Its breath is hot and rains down on me each time it opens its mouth. Still, I don't move and I refuse to release him from my glare. "Go home!" It's a yelled thought that pierces into its thick skull. I feel the exact moment it hears and acknowledges my words.

Sharp pains sear through my body until I want to scream in agony.

Then the creature wavers, takes a step back, its mouth closing partially, the vicious roaring ceasing. I feel someone behind me then I see Jake's outstretched arms as he pushes the creature back into the forest.

For endless seconds we wait for it to reappear but it doesn't and inside I smile. I did it.

"He's gone home," I proclaim.

"For good?" Sasha asks.

I nod. "For good. He won't come back unless he's summoned again."

But the dark of night still looms. Above, the moon is pushing its way over the sun so that now there's just a slither of light emanating from an otherwise dark orb.

"That's the solar corona," Jake says.

We all stand there and I wonder if they're feeling the same thing I am. It's like my body is filling up. From the bottom to the top like someone pouring water into a glass. I stand perfectly still being consumed and reborn. A glance to the side shows the others standing perfectly still, as well.

Then they rush forward, the demon shadows charge us. They have no eyes so I cannot link to any of them. They're fast and knock me and Sasha down almost instantly. Jake can outrun them, and when he turns back around he uses his power to push them deep into the trees. They come right back.

Krystal raises both her arms, her head's held back, long dark hair flowing in the breeze. She looks exotic and ethereal as the blue from her mark lights the dark clearing. From the ground rises white shadowy silhouettes that all hover head-first in her direction as if they're waiting for her next command. Lifting her head she stares at them and with a wave of her arms, sends them to attack the demon shadows.

While the wind howls around us, fierce screams of battle echo through the trees.

"The spirits will take care of the demons," Krystal announces.

"We just have to find him," Sasha says.

Jake nods. "I know where he is."

"How do you know?" I ask.

"I can feel him. He's been in my head taunting me all the time you took out the creature. He's waiting for our failure, watching from the sidelines like a coward. Well, we're taking this fight right to him!" Jake says and starts walking in a westerly direction, deeper into the forest.

Without another word we follow behind him, trekking through trees and darkness once again. My chest is pounding from all of our adrenaline combined, my fingers tingle with power and my eyes scan the forest as we move through. I don't know what I'm looking for, I just know that something's out there and I don't want to be caught off guard when that something decides to show its face.

It's just us now, I can tell, our Guardians aren't here and neither is Fatima. We're walking this journey by ourselves because this is the way it was meant to be. I'm no longer intimidated by that thought. In the back of my mind I see my parents' faces. Their smiles and their encouragement push me forward. I know I'm doing exactly what they would have wanted me to do.

When I think we've walked to the other side of Lincoln, at least, Jake stops. I don't know what keeps us from all bumping into each other, but instead we're spread apart, each looking around. The only light we have is the golden ray of the solar corona still peeking from around the eclipse. It's seeping through the tops of trees falling on the ground in golden spears. But I can feel that Jake is standing just ahead of us, Sasha and Krystal are to my left and right, respectively. We're all alert, waiting, expecting.

The ground between us suddenly falls out, like an earthquake centralized in one spot, dirt and debris fall away leaving a big black hole. And just when we get ready to take a step to see what's at the bottom of the hole, a funnel of black smoke erupts. I fall back, coughing, choking from the thick smoke. I hear the others doing the same. With the smoke comes that sick, demented laughter. Using an arm to shield my eyes I struggle to stay on my feet. If Charon has made his appearance, I want to see him. I want to look this demon right in the eyes and send him back to Hades where he belongs!

But he has no eyes.

He rises, his body covered by a hooded black cloak that billows in the wind. Taller and taller, he surpasses us and almost the tips of the trees. The smoke swirls around his feet in huge waves.

"Finally, the Mystyx come to meet their fate."

The ground beneath me trembles and I almost fall. The wind seems to have picked up so that leaves and branches and whatever else is not nailed down in the forest is being hurled at us.

"Styx was a fool to ever think kids could banish me. A fool!" he yells and the wind howls behind his voice like background music.

I don't know what to do. I mean, this is what we were meant for, what our whole purpose in this life is and I don't know how to handle it. I can't influence the mind of a demon with no eyes. I don't know if Jake can move this monstrosity of an entity or if Krystal's ghost army can push him back into this hole he came out of. I just don't know.

At my sides my fingers shake but I refuse to run, refuse to back down.

"He can't win." Fatima's voice floats on the air.

I look around but I know I won't see her.

"Stand strong together, the four of you, with Styx. He cannot win against you."

And I don't know how much longer I can stand up, I feel like I'm in the center of a tornado. Something's on my arm, grabbing for me and I'm afraid it might be something coming from Charon's smoke stance, but it's not. It's Sasha.

"Take my hand!" she screams.

It's a struggle but I manage to twine my fingers with hers. On my other side Jake comes up and grips my hands. Only because all of our marks are glowing do I know that Krystal is on Sasha's other side. We're standing together, all of us focusing every bit of energy we have on Charon, but nothing happens.

He laughs again and lifts one arm to point down at us. "You still do not believe. I am all powerful! It is my destiny to rule!"

"It is your destiny to die, Charon!" Jake yells in return and tries to use his strength to push the demon back.

Charon's body sways with the motion but does not yield. He stands straighter and laughs louder. "No, Mystyx! It is your destiny to die!"

And as he says those words the sky crackles and seems to split open with fierce golden streaks of lightning. Those belts rain down around us, spearing the ground and setting mini fires until we're completely surrounded.

"What do we do now?" Sasha screams. "What do we do?"

Krystal opens her mouth, about to say something, then closes it quickly. But it's her eyes I'm really following. She's thinking something knows the answer. It's just been spoken to her by someone or some spirit. She reaches into her jacket pocket and pulls out her river stones. With a slow smile she holds her palm out for all of us to see.

Charon waves his hand so that the small fires rise higher, swirling into a funnel of fire around us. The heat is what I feel first and foremost, burning my skin until I think it's going to peel right off. It's bright here, the fire is so intense we all look like we're glowing.

Sasha pulls her stones from the cell phone case at her hip where she'd been keeping them since Mrs. Hampton gave them to us.

"Hurry!" she yells and her face starts to look distorted, like the fire's burning her features away.

I dig into my back pocket and grab my stones pulling my hand out and thrusting my palm forward. We all look to Jake then because we don't really know if he has his stones or not. Mrs. Hampton only gave us ours, saying that Jake would receive his when the time was right. Well, I guess now would be as good a time as any.

But Jake doesn't have anything.

I see it in his eyes.

"Your Guardian should have given them to you!" Krystal

yells. "Didn't he give them to you?" Jake is about to shake his head no when the ground shifts again.

My feet are sinking, the ground is like quicksand now with Charon's fire above us, the demon himself laughing and predicting our doom.

Jake lifts his hand into the air. If I didn't know better I'd swear he was reaching up to take a handful of fire. Instead he yells, "Stones!"

And through the wall of fire falls four stones, landing precisely into Jake's hand. We don't question it, there's no time. We look at each other and with a nod all drop our stones onto the sinking ground at the same time. Then we hurry and grasp hands once more, closing our eyes and praying for the best.

The explosion is loud, it shakes us until we're all falling, hands still clasped. My eyes are closed and I think we're falling down that black hole. Dying, I think. Dying young, just like that song I love so much.

I want to be buried in roses. I want them all around me, in all different shades. I want soft music, soft lights…if I die young.

twenty-eight

And The Cursed Shall Fall

It doesn't hurt. This falling and falling, doesn't hurt at all. What does hurt is wondering what if?

What if we'd beat Charon?

What if we were really strong enough, powerful enough to save the world?

What if my parents had lived?

What if Dylan had lived?

I open my eyes and the "what ifs" disappear. It's beautiful, like fireworks shooting into the sky on the Fourth of July. We're still in this funnel but it's not of fire anymore, it's of light. At the top of the funnel is where the fireworks spark and soar in brilliant colors. It's loud and then it's not. Like the sound is there but it's so soft against my ears I think I'm imagining it all.

Tearing my gaze away from the spectacular lights I look for my friends, my partners in this journey. And they're all there. Krystal, her blue tone haloing her, Sasha in her all her pink glory and Jake, looking handsome and bold in his green. We're all here—the Mystyx.

Now, if I only knew where "here" was.

"You have done well, my children."

There's another voice—there always seems to be a voice, either in my head or on the air, so many beings speaking to us now.

"You, the chosen, have done well. Charon's curse is complete. He is for all time banished from the realms."

"Styx, the goddess," I whisper but it sounds like I've yelled it into a bullhorn.

"My little empath. You were very brave to bid Lor goodbye," she says and if I weren't already in a cone of light I'd probably beam.

"All of you are brave and strong. The Vortex, the medium and the traveler I am proud to say you are mine."

We smile at each other about two seconds before we're falling again. This time it's a quick fall and an even quicker plop to the ground that is thankfully now solid.

"Wow." Krystal speaks first.

Sasha chuckles. "Yeah, wow."

Not only is the ground hard but the wind has stopped whipping everything in sight. There's no black smoke, no shadows. Just us and the forest. And it's simply…wow.

Beside me I scoop up my stones and put them back into my pocket before standing. "Was that it?"

Jake's holding his stones in his palm shaking them a little so they're making a clinking sound. "I think so."

"All this time all we had to do was drop some rocks and he'd vanish?" Sasha asks. "Strange and unexpected."

"I think it was more than that. I mean, I think we had to do more. We had to grow and to experience things that would test us, make us stronger," I say.

"I agree," Krystal speaks up, brushing her tangled hair

back from her face. "We had to own our powers and to trust each other. We did that tonight. We stood together and he couldn't touch us. He couldn't stop us."

"So we win this time." Jake grabs Krystal's hand and kisses her forehead.

Sasha and I look at each other, then quickly away. It's too painful to look at Krystal and Jake, at the love they share.

"Now it's over," Sasha snaps. "We can go home."

She starts to walk ahead of us. Jake and Krystal only stare at her. I figure that's my cue.

"I'll catch up with her," I tell them and give them their privacy.

A chilly rain starts to fall tickling my skin and clearing the air of the burnt acrid stench. As I'm walking beside Sasha now I feel what she's feeling—the anger, the disappointment, the heartbreak. I feel it and recognize it and with a start realize it's because most of those feelings are mine, as well. She wants to graduate, to move away from Lincoln and start a new life. I do, too. I'm glad we did what we were supposed to do, happy that we all survived. But at the same time I'm relieved that this duty has been lifted from us, from me. I'm ready to live my life on my own terms and by my own rules. It's fine that I have the mark of the Mystyx on my ankle. I'll wear it proudly. But as for the rest, my job is done. I'm moving on because if I don't, I'm afraid I won't survive.

twenty-nine

Welcome Back, I Think…

Krystal

IT'S him.

He's not dead.

Franklin is alive.

Even though I can't see his eyes I know it's him. His body is a little different, broader, I think. His clothes are not the same—the Seven "A" pocket jeans and fitted True Religion T-shirt a one-eighty turn from his old khakis and polo shirts. Still, I know it's him. And I know that he's looking at me.

I'm all tingly inside standing here at the edge of the forest, a chilly wind blowing against my skin. Charon is banished, he's never coming back. We did it. The Mystyx conquered the evil darkness before it could envelop the world.

But I'm not reveling in the victory with the others. I'm standing here looking at him, wondering what…when… how…it is he's here after all this time.

I'd seen him in my dreams, more times than I wanted

to remember. I heard his voice, felt his fingers brush across my skin when nobody was visibly around. I watched him disappear in a cloud of black smoke almost a year ago. And yet…he's here, not ten feet away from me.

"Hey, Krystal," he says, the left side of his mouth lifting in a half grin.

"Hey," I finally manage and can't for the life of me think of what else to say.

I have a boyfriend, comes to mind. But he didn't ask me that.

Where have you been, is a good question. But I'm not sure I really want to know.

He lifts a hand and touches the side of his sunglasses, pulling them down slightly so I can see his eyes. They look just like they used to, then they don't. They're red.

"See ya around," he says then gives me a full-toothed smile before turning and disappearing into the woods.

★ ★ ★ ★ ★

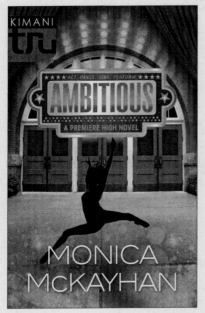